The Silk Road

By

Douglas Pacheco

Illustrated by
Amy Cullings Moreno

Published by Pen It! Publications, LLC in the U.S.A.
812-371-4128   www.penitpublications.com

ISBN: 978-1-954004-11-5

Illustrated by Amy Cullings Moreno

All Scriptural References are from The New American Standard Bible unless otherwise noted.

Dedication

To children everywhere who know, without anyone telling them, that they were made for a great purpose.

You will not find adventure by hiding in your room or taking the easy way. The calling of God is not easy. It was meant to be hard. Great adventure lies in going after the hard things…even the seemingly impossible things because; when you do, a God of miracles shows up.

The Great Adventure awaits you, my friend. Obey the calling in your heart. Even if no one else wants to follow, go out and blaze new trails, swim against the current, and listen to the quiet voice leading you to the one road …the only road.

Be courageous and find the *Silk Road…*
It is just there…just beyond your front yard.

Introduction

This is a children's book, but in reality, it is a parable for all ages about discovery and the journey that discovery requires.

As children, we learn about our world first through the love and care of our family. Their care and nurturing bring each of us to the place where we can begin asking the constant question that has been placed within every human being upon the earth:

"Who am I and why am I here?"

In this parable, two small caterpillars, miracles in their own right, Fearful and Hopeful begin a transformative journey to answer that question for themselves. Like them, we ALL, from birth, sojourn through the events that happen in our lives that lead us to some amazing discoveries, among which are:

1. We are not in control of our lives, even though we think we are.

2. Along the journey, fear and obstacles will try to keep us from moving forward, so that we will quit and not discover our purpose.

3. Overcoming the fear, the obstacles and dangers along the way is what brings us into maturity. It shows us what lies in our hearts, and where we discover the work of *Wonderful*.

Parables are told because we humans make things too complicated. Jesus said:
> *"Let the little children come to me, and do not hinder them, for the kingdom of heaven belongs to such as these." Matthew 19:14 NIV*

What the world is looking for is the simple, pure truth. When Jesus walked the earth, He told this truth through parables…much like the one you are about to read.

Whether you are nine or ninety years old, you will recognize yourself in this story, and my hope is that you will once again, for the first time, know the meaning of the Scripture in Isaiah 9:6,

"For a child is born to us, a son is given to us. The government will rest on his shoulders. And he will be called: **Wonderful** *Counselor, Mighty God, Everlasting Father, Prince of Peace. His government and its peace will never end."*

Douglas Pacheco

Table of Contents

Chapter One

The Journey

Fearful awakened that day feeling something was different. The sky was as blue as it had ever been, and the sun was bright and warm, as it usually was on every fall day. But today was peculiar and he didn't know why. The aura of some odd feeling filled the atmosphere.

Caterpillars generally get up and have a wonderful breakfast of milkweed and mint tea, then go out to see some friends, but not on this day. This morning was the first time in his short life that Fearful had an intense desire to travel.

He couldn't explain WHY he felt this way. It was as if a switch had flipped on inside of him or a button had been pushed. Fearful had heard that the other caterpillars felt the urge to take a long trip, but he never understood it…until today!

Stepping out into the bright sun, he made his way to the home of his friend, Hopeful, who was out in his garden tending his milkweed. Most caterpillars like to sit for hours, conversing quietly with friends, or like Hopeful, tending their gardens and minding their business.

Fearful approached his friend's fence, he was still so overwhelmed by the urge to take a trip that he didn't even say good morning. Instead, he said, "Hopeful, I awakened this morning with the most curious feeling I have ever felt…the feeling of wanting to take a long trip."

Hopeful was happy to see his friend, and upon the mention of a long trip, Hopeful's eyes lit up. He turned quickly and looked into Fearful's rather cloudy eyes and said, "I awakened with the same, desire my friend!"

The two laughed nervously, explaining to each other how curious it was that something inside of them had just been awakened. They were filled with excitement and Fearful said, "I must return home immediately and begin packing…I must pack and pack and pack…one mustn't be too careful when packing!"

They agreed to meet the next morning to begin their journey into the unknown. Fearful returned home and removed his silk backpack from his closet and began packing EVERYTHING he could possibly need.

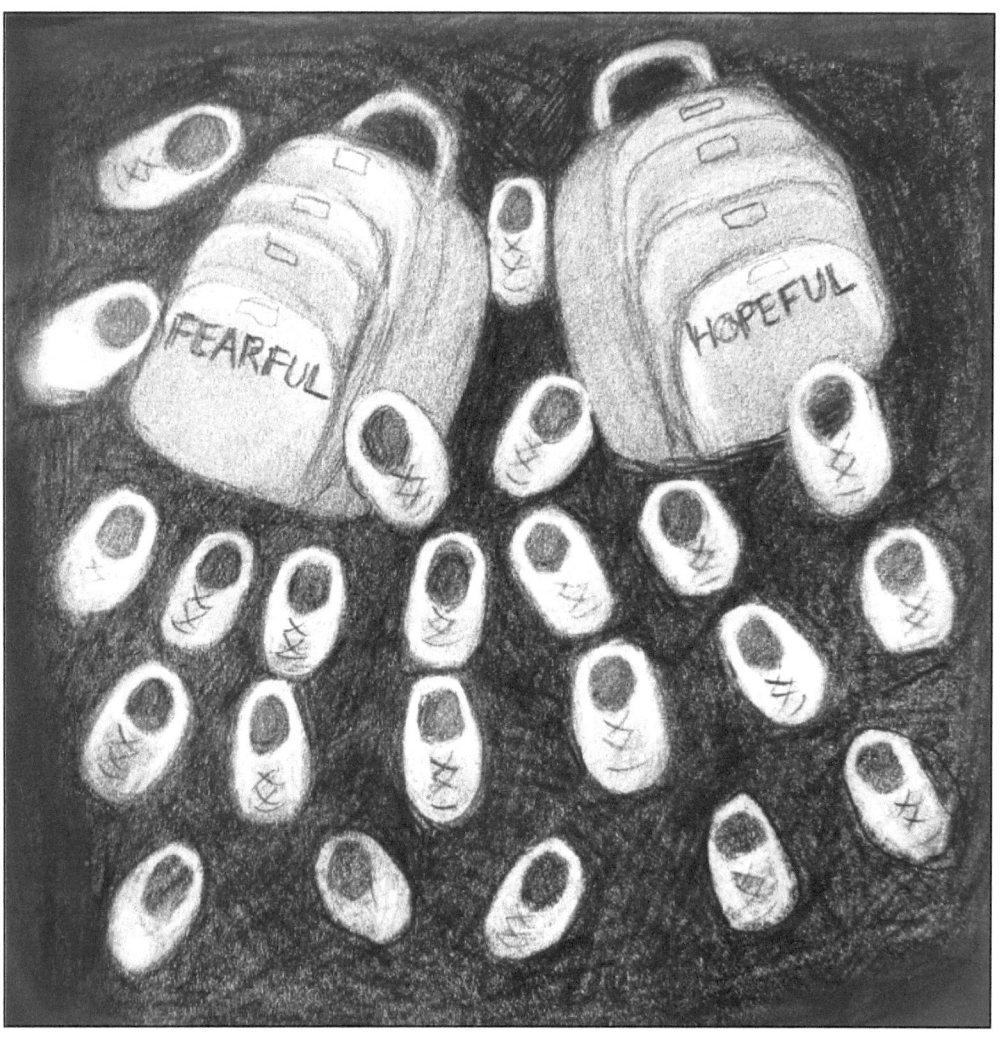

He packed all the food in his small house, and every pair of socks in his drawer (which are a lot of socks, since caterpillars have sixteen feet!) He took all the sweaters, shirts, vests and hats he found in the drawer (Fearful did this because he believed if he prepared for anything that could happen, it would give him comfort and security). The backpack was so heavy, he could barely lift it.

The next morning, Fearful arrived at Hopeful's house, tugging along his heavy silk backpack. Hopeful, on the other hand, had packed very lightly, taking only the food he would need for the next day and fresh socks for his sixteen little feet. Hopeful knew that whatever need that might arise during the journey, the answer would be found along the way.

Looking at Fearful's backpack, Hopeful realized his friend would need help carrying it. He lifted the other side of Fearful's backpack and they started on their journey.

"Where are we going Hopeful?" Fearful asked, nervously.

"We are beginning our journey, my dear friend," Hopeful replied.

"But how do you know where we are going?" Fearful asked, wringing four of his feet.

Hopeful replied, "No one KNOWS exactly where they are going. It's only when you begin the journey that the way becomes clear, and with time, it becomes even clearer."

This seemed reasonable to Fearful. They walked through the yard and onto the Dandelion Trail, where all the garden insects walked. Fearful had tied double knots in all sixteen of his tennis shoes. He hoped this would help him feel more confident on his journey.

As they walked, many of the other insects asked them where they were going. They explained, and the insects looked at them as if they were very strange, indeed.

"Why would you want to leave your home and go somewhere else?" [1] the crickets asked.

"Why would you want to leave your friends, your land, your houses, and your family behind?" the stink bugs asked.

Hopeful smiled his bravest smile and said, "Sometimes change simply means we must leave a place we know and go to one where we have never been, to explore new and exciting opportunities. But…" he continued, pulling his shoulders back, "once we take the first step, courage fills us and we begin to discover who we were really created to be!"

All the insects wished them a good journey and waved as they walked into the distance.

They traveled the entire day until the sun fell low in the sky., They looked for the tallest stalk of Queen Anne's lace they could find. They climbed to the top and rested. They talked about what they would find on the road ahead, until at last, they fell fast asleep.

Chapter Two

The Shallow Pool

The next morning, Hopeful and Fearful came to the end of the Dandelion Trail. They entered a stretch of overgrown grass known to all the other insects as, "The Field." To the right of the barely visible path was a broken, weathered sign that read, "The Silk Road…trade route to The Beautiful Valley." This was not territory they had ever visited before. There was no well-worn path here like they had found on the Dandelion Trail.

Fearful felt afraid this morning. He still had the desire to travel, but today his thoughts were centered on what trouble lay ahead, instead of looking forward to where the road would lead them. This was very odd, indeed. Fearful wondered what the part of the sign meant that said, "trade route to the Beautiful Valley."

"Trade what?" asked an inquisitive Fearful. "I have nothing I wish to trade," he said to Hopeful.

Hopeful smiled. "I have heard of the Silk Road. An ancient trade route joining East and West," he said, hoping to quell Fearful's anxiety. "Travelers would trade the goods they had for others they wished to have."

"You are correct!" said a voice in the top of the grassy forest. It was Mantis. "However," continued Mantis, "you will discover, my small friends, that you are mistaken if you believe you have nothing to trade! The Silk Road will show you what you must trade in exchange for the privilege of continuing to the Beautiful Valley. Many begin, but very few finish the Silk Road."

Fearful asked, "Why is it called, 'The SILK Road?'"

Mantis sat quietly for a moment, considering whether or not Fearful would be able to understand his answer. He finally spoke.

"It is called the SILK Road because you enter poor and leave rich," said Mantis. "You start on the road with your fears and your failures and they are transformed into the rich silk of courage, honor and wisdom.

These traits make the garments of kings!"

Fearful looked at Hopeful and then back at the sign. "Lead on Hopeful...I think have everything I need to make it to the Beautiful Valley right here in my silk backpack!"

Hopeful thanked Mantis and they moved forward.

A short distance later along the Silk Road, they came to a shallow pool of water formed from the light rain the night before. They discovered they could not go around it, but rather, they had to go through it. This was easy for Hopeful since he had not brought much with him on his journey. He went through it easily, and came safely to the other side.

Fearful was in a great panic. "I cannot pass through the water without the risk of losing everything I have brought with me!" He was distressed, as he went through one motion and then another, trying all he could to keep his silk backpack contents safe and dry.

Fearful was angry that Hopeful wasn't helping him cross through the shallow pool. "Why will you not wait to help me to cross through the water!?" Fearful asked, angrily.

Hopeful sighed! He knew when he had seen the overstuffed backpack that Fearful was going to have trouble along the way. He spoke gently to his friend. "Fearful, each of us must carry what we have brought with us. I cannot carry your load, and you, my friend, cannot carry mine. We must each find our own way through." Hopeful smiled reassuringly to his little friend.

After exhausting all other possibilities, Fearful resolved he must go through the same way Hopeful did. As he entered the water, his sandwiches, mint tea, and all he had brought with him fell out of the backpack and sank to the bottom of the slow-moving water. They were lost in the shallow pool. Fearful sat by the side of the shallow pool feeling defeated.

"You have emerged a different caterpillar than the one who entered the other side,"[2] said Hopeful. "You have just traded trusting what you brought in your silk backpack for passage through the shallow pool."

Fearful understood what Mantis had meant when he said, *"The Silk Road will show you what you must trade in exchange for the privilege of continuing to the Beautiful Valley."*

Hopeful's words did not encourage Fearful one bit, because he was sad to have lost everything he trusted in. Fearful was now in possession of his empty silk backpack. He found that he did have a small portion of watered-down mint tea left.

Fearful felt vulnerable, and said to Hopeful with a shaky voice, "I want to go back to our yard, Hopeful."

Hopeful cautioned his young friend, "What has been left in the water are just remnants of your old life, my friend. If you return, you will still remain empty-handed…even what you have left after going through the shallow pool is useless to you now! Besides, if you go back now, the great journey we've set out upon will remain a mystery to you, as well.[3] If you continue with me, not only will you regain what you have lost in the shallow pool, but you will have the opportunity to see how all your needs will be provided for!"

Now with only nine of his sixteen tennis shoes, (the others were stuck in the mud at the bottom of the shallow pool), Fearful stumbled forward, more fearful than ever, wondering why he ever began this journey in the first place.

Chapter 3
The Crows

The two traveled on for quite some time talking. Fearful opined the loss of his beloved tennis shoes and the contents of his backpack. After a little time had passed, they sat down to dry out their clothes, shoes, and backpacks, and to eat a little before continuing.

A dragonfly droned overhead, asking for directions to the shallow pool. Hopeful obliged with the directions and the dragonfly flew on.

The pair felt a curious movement of the earth around them. At first, Fearful thought it was an earthquake. An earthworm stuck his head up out of the dirt a short distance in front of them.

"Oh, how I hate having to crawl under the ground," said the earthworm. "How is it that I have to burrow under the ground and you two are fortunate enough to be crawling on the top of it?"

Fearful and Hopeful looked at one another and grinned.

The earthworm continued, "All my life," he paused, wiping the mud out of his eyes, "having to go around rocks, living in mud and hiding from birds…you don't know how lucky you are," he complained to the caterpillars.

Hopeful smiled and bowed to the earthworm. "Mister earthworm, what profit is there to complain of the circumstances we find ourselves in? Unlike you, we can be seen by any enemy who wants to eat us up, but you remain hidden underground. Do you now see your good fortune?"

The earthworm simply continued, as if he hadn't heard what was said, and kept complaining and murmuring about having to live in the dirt. A dark shadow suddenly swept over the ground where they stood talking. Hopeful's instincts told him that they must hide in the grass forest in The Field. When he looked up into the sky, he saw a murder of crows that was seeking a meal!

Fearful also saw the crows and shook nervously. He complained to Hopeful, "We should never have come on this trip! We were safe in our yard, our comfort zone. We had friends, and there were no pools in our yard and NO CROWS!"

Hopeful crouched quietly, saying nothing. He kept his eyes fixed on the crows overhead, which puzzled Fearful and he began to repeat the same speech. Hopeful placed his tiny caterpillar foot over Fearful's mouth.

"Shhhh!" he said, pointing upward.

Fearful saw a crow circling overhead. Speaking in a very low voice, Hopeful warned him, "Be very careful what you say with your mouth, my young friend. Crows can hear murmuring and complaining and can zero in on it like radar…they circle in until they find the source of the sound. Complaining and murmuring is a delicacy to the crows!" [4]

The earthworm continued on, complaining so much that he was not even aware that Hopeful and Fearful had taken cover in the grass forest a few yards away. The earthworm did not see the dark shadows looming larger and larger over him. He was so concerned with his own lot in life, and consumed with self-pity, he was unaware of the danger.

Fearful whispered to the earthworm, "Sir, please look above you! Look up!"

But the earthworm could only hear his own complaining.

A crow silently swooped down and gobbled up the earthworm! Fearful's eyes grew large and he was so afraid that he felt paralyzed with fear. Hopeful remained still and quiet.

The crow stood, looking slowly in all directions, after finishing off the earthworm. He stared intently into the grass forest. Fearful and Hopeful remained completely still and then, just as quickly as he had come, the crow lifted back into the air.

After a few moments, Fearful whispered, "Are we safe?"

Hopeful smiled reassuringly, "Yes, but do not complain again, Fearful, to complain is to invite the very thing you fear to carry you away!" [5]

Chapter 4
The Pill Bugs

After the crows had flown away, the two came out of their hiding place in the grass forest and Fearful began looking into his silk backpack for something to eat. (Fearful always ate when he was nervous or afraid.) As he searched, he saw what he thought was some sort of *writing* on the inside of his backpack. Upon closer observation, Fearful saw it was indeed writing, but it was written in backward and upside down letters. He could not understand the writing.

Surprised by his discovery, Fearful said to Hopeful, "My backpack is defective! There is writing in it. The writing is backwards and I cannot make out the words!"

Hopeful told him that *his* backpack also had writing in it that he couldn't understand either, but not to worry about it. "There are far too many things that we CAN understand, to worry about the ones we cannot"

They were confused about the writing inside their bags. Hopeful tried to continue the conversation so Fearful would not dwell on the crows. As they continued their journey into the field, Fearful asked, "How do we defend ourselves? The earthworm was so easy for the crow to eat. What can we do to stay safe?"

Hopeful knew there would be danger on their trip, and had intended to talk to Fearful before they started their journey, but decided against it. He had learned in the great assembly of caterpillars, called the *Congregation of the Clan*, about the protection of *Wonderful*, their protector. Fearful had never been in the Congregation of the Clan and had no knowledge of this. He thought it best to let Fearful learn as they went along.

Hopeful raised his head, and stood erect, as he began to answer Fearful's question. Before he could answer, they walked into a clearing and stumbled upon a group of pill bugs, shooting pool, and using one another as the cue ball and pool balls. Upon seeing the travelers, the pill bugs invited them to visit.

The two caterpillars laughed, as they were welcomed into the pill bug's camp. Watching them shoot pool, Fearful soon forgot about their previous trouble with the crows and relaxed. The sun in the sky began to go down, and as the evening approached swiftly, Hopeful made a small campfire. The caterpillars and pill bugs began to discuss the caterpillars' journey.

"You are two brave caterpillars to be walking The Field all by yourselves!" stated one of the pill bugs.

"Have you not heard that the crows are out there, looking for tasty meals?" asked another.

Fearful looked sideways at Hopeful, waiting to see what he would reply. Hopeful instead, tried to deflect any other questions that would fill his friend with fear until he could speak with him about *Wonderful.*

"How do YOU defend yourselves?" Fearful asked, with raised eyebrows. He was hoping to learn ways to protect themselves on their journey.

The oldest of the pill bugs explained that their defense mechanism against attackers was to roll up tightly into a ball, so that nothing could hurt them.

"We have a strong armor to keep us from being injured!"

"You mean, NOTHING can hurt you?" Fearful asked.

"Well," boasted another pill bug, "so far, nothing has been able to pierce our protective shells, so we aren't afraid of anything!"

Fearful was envious. He resented having no hard, outer shell to protect himself. Hopeful could tell that his vulnerability bothered him very much.

After discussing how they protected themselves, one of the pill bugs asked Fearful and Hopeful, "What is *your* defense mechanism?"

Fearful was taken off guard by this question. He could tell the pill bugs were looking at he and Hopeful to tell them an equally impressive story. He was embarrassed by the fact that they had no story to tell. Hopeful tried to change the subject, but the pill bugs continued to ask the caterpillars how they defended themselves. After thinking for quite some time and feeling increasingly embarrassed by not having an answer to the pill bugs' incessant questions, Fearful's pride got the best of him. He didn't want the pill bugs to think less of caterpillars, and so he decided to make up a story.[6]

"We have SECRET horns that come out of our heads and SECRET claws that come out of our feet too!"

This impressed them, and the caterpillars could hear "Oooh" and "Ahhh!' and "Wow!" from the pill bugs. Fearful felt proud because of their affirmation. Hopeful rolled his eyes at Fearful, who shrugged his shoulders and sheepishly grinned. The pill bugs now looked at the caterpillars with great esteem, and for a short while, all seemed well until one of them, the smallest asked, "Let us see your horns then!"[7]

Fearful's eyes got big and he looked at the ground, uncomfortable because he hadn't anticipated that the pill bugs would want to see proof of his boast. Hopeful decided to sit back and let Fearful figure out the price for lying.

Finally, Fearful said, "They only come out when we're raving mad!" thinking that this added lie would be enough for the pill bugs.

This only encouraged the two smallest pill bugs, who had been acting like pool balls, to begin rolling hard into Fearful and Hopeful to trying to make them angry.

Fearful said, "You had better stop before I get angry!"

But this made them roll even harder into them. Hopeful realized Fearful's lie now affected his own safety, because the pill bugs eventually knocked him down. They bumped into Hopeful and bent his antenna until it hurt.

"STOP," said the June bug, who had been sitting unseen next to the edge of the grass forest. "Caterpillars HAVE no defense mechanism!" she said with authority.

The pill bugs looked puzzled at the June bug, at one another and then, turned to Fearful. The smallest pill bug, confused, began, "But you said…"

"I know what he said," Hopeful interrupted, hoping to intercede. He looked sternly at Fearful. "When a caterpillar becomes afraid of what others may think of him, he makes up silly stories and tries to sound more important than he is. Fearful was embarrassed to tell you that we have no visible defense mechanism like your armor or like Miss June Bug with her hard shell… we have no horns either."

"No antlers?" asked the pill bugs.

"No antlers!" said Hopeful.

"No claws? No stinger?"

"No…no claws, no stinger, no poisonous tail or pinchers…"

Little by little, a giggle rose among the smaller pill bugs and turned into outright howls. Soon, all the bugs around the fire were laughing hysterically. Hopeful chuckled a little, and then joined the pill bugs, because he saw how silly it was to lie. Fearful hung his head and looked down at the ground, feeling so embarrassed.

The June bug, who had still been quiet during the laughter, looked at Fearful and asked out loud, "Do you, my friend, not know that *Wonderful* is your protector?"

The pill bugs gasped and stopped laughing when the June bug mentioned the name of *Wonderful*. Fearful looked puzzled.

The June bug continued, "Some of us have been given armor for protection, but for those who have not received this gift, a greater and more powerful protection has been given to them…by *Wonderful* Himself!"

The June bug looked curiously at Fearful, as one looks with surprise at those who do not know they are special. Fearful did not understand what she meant by that statement.

The June bug said, "Those who seem the most vulnerable, and the least powerful…these are the ones who have the personal protection of *Wonderful*…He is their shield!"

Hopeful could see that Fearful was going to ask June bug what she meant so he interrupted the conversation with a fake yawn. The June bug and Hopeful looked at one another, and the June bug understood at that moment that Fearful had not yet met *Wonderful* or known of His ways . Hopeful smiled a grateful smile to the June bug and nodded appreciatively.

The fire began dying down and the pill bugs, sufficiently tired from the laughter and activity of the evening, yawned from exhaustion.

"We must sleep…we have a long journey to continue tomorrow," Hopeful said., Fearful walked silently, a few steps behind his wiser friend. The caterpillars bid goodnight to the group and went into the grass forest atop a tall stalk of Queen Anne's lace to sleep.

Chapter 5
The Army

Fearful silently fumed with anger as they reached the top of the Queen Anne's lace, because he was so embarrassed. There were many questions to ask, but he knew he had to think things through before he spoke with Hopeful again.

When morning dawned the next day, Fearful and Hopeful crawled down from their safe perch and continued their journey. Hopeful told Fearful he had heard from others that all caterpillars went to the Beautiful Valley, where they underwent a profound *Changing*. Fearful was still silent and listened to Hopeful, but was still troubled by the events of the previous evening.

Not too far along on their journey that day, they heard a sound like distant thunder. As the ground began to shake, Hopeful told Fearful to get into the top of the Queen Anne's lace. It was a hard climb for Fearful because his remaining tennis shoes kept slipping off. He quickly removed them and climbed the Queen Anne's lace with ease, once his old tennis shoes were gone. They had just made it up, when an entire legion of ants came pounding through the path, consuming anything and everything in their way.

Safe atop their stalk, Hopeful and Fearful went unnoticed by the ants, but were shocked by what they saw. The pill bugs, who had been confident in their defenses, were no match for the ants.[8] Even though they had rolled into little balls, the big pinchers of the ants easily picked them up, and carried them away to be food for their queen.

As the caterpillars watched in disbelief, the little pill bug who had begun rolling into Fearful happened to look up and see Fearful and Hopeful in the

Queen Anne's lace. He mouthed some words, but Fearful couldn't hear them. He couldn't understand how with their strong armor the pill bugs were still not safe. This bothered Fearful quite a bit.

He wondered to himself, 'How can anyone be safe if their armor isn't strong enough to protect them?'

Hours and hours passed as the caterpillars watched the army of ants take all the creatures they had captured back to their nest. Lady bugs, grasshoppers, pill bugs, and even a lizard were being carried back to their nest. Fearful looked on with big eyes. He had never been so afraid.

Later, after the ants were long gone, Fearful sat atop their place of safety, but could no longer keep silent. He looked at Hopeful and demanded answers.

"Why is the journey so dangerous? And the pill bugs," Fearful continued, becoming angrier as he spoke, "they were all taken away by the Ants! They said they were safe from everything! If they aren't safe, how will we ever make it to our destination?"

Fearful's voice became panicked and the questions just poured out like water. His fear had clouded his heart and his mind so much that he could no longer control his anger.

"Why did the pill bugs' armor not protect them? Why is all of this happening? How are we to get to where we're going? What did June bug mean when she said, *Wonderful* is your protector?'"

Question after question after question. Panic continued to fill his eyes and desperation came over him. Hopeful tried calming him down, but Fearful would not listen because of his despair.

At last, he blurted out in anger, "I am not taking another step until I understand everything!" Then he burst into tears.

Hopeful, for the moment, stayed quiet. He knew it was impossible to reason with fear.

Fearful became angry when Hopeful remained silent and said shouted at him, "I should never have come with you! All you do is say, 'Good things are coming and something good is around the corner,' but you don't know what exactly it is!" Because he was so afraid, Fearful had allowed his fear to turn him against his best friend.

After a long silence, Hopeful spoke up quietly, saying, "My dear friend, you are not able to see what is ahead because you are allowing fear to rule your mind and heart." Then gathering his courage and speaking in a very measured and confident tone he said, "Your desire to be safe is understandable, Fearful, but you must trade the desire to be safe for courage, or it will keep you from discovering your higher purpose, my friend." He continued, "Never sacrifice your purpose for personal safety or pleasure, Fearful, or you'll lose both!" Hopeful finished, "There are some things more important than safety, my friend. The June bug was right," he explained.

"*Wonderful is* our protector!"

Hopeful then addressed Fearful's question. "I do know, deep down in my heart, I *know* that what is ahead is for our good!" Fearful looked at Hopeful as he continued, "Around this corner or the next is a reward so great that we cannot see or even imagine it. I have heard this from others who have gone before us, and in my heart, I know it is true!" he said with conviction, and then he became silent once again.

The crickets could be heard playing their violins in the moonlight, and the fireflies gave off a soft glow in the darkness, showcasing its beauty. The world was quiet and peaceful for the time being. Fearful had been trembling and sobbing, as he listened to his friend. He looked at Hopeful with tears in his eyes. He felt deeply sorry for his hurtful words and his lies the previous night with the pill bugs, but all that he could do now was to muster one feeble question.

"What *is* around the corner, Hopeful?" he asked, not quite sure he wanted an answer to his question.

"There's something," Hopeful answered, "but there is much fog and I can't see what exactly it is…I think it might be... that is to say, I believe it may be...*Wonderful*!"

Fearful's eyes grew large and he asked, "What if it isn't?"

"Well," Hopeful said confidently, "we will keep going until *Wonderful* shows up. He always shows up and He brings lots of new things with

Him."

Fearful asked timidly, "Are they scary things?"

Hopeful smiled and said, "All things that *Wonderful* brings appear scary at first." Biting his lower lip, he continued, "But once you get past the newness and scariness, *wonderfulness* starts coming out of them to make our lives abundant and special! You have to take the chance, Fearful, otherwise wonderfulness will happen without you!"

Fearful asked the question Hopeful had been anticipating: "Who is this …*Wonderful?* Is he a caterpillar, like us?"

There was a rustling in the grass forest and both Fearful and Hopeful crouched down low atop the Queen Anne's lace. Hopeful squinted through the darkness and looked intently in the direction of the noise, wondering what could be coming. Fearful closed his eyes tightly. He didn't want to believe something else dangerous was happening. Hopeful looked over the edge of their perch, and a smile lit up his face.

Fearful saw the smile, and because he always ate when he was nervous, asked, "What do you see, Hopeful? A milkweed sandwich?" (Caterpillars *love* milkweed sandwiches!)

Out of the dense thickness of the grass forest appeared another caterpillar, just like them!

He was an older caterpillar with kind eyes. Hopeful recognized at once that this was the guide he had learned about in the Congregation of the Clan, known to caterpillars as 'Helper.' [10, 11] As he came walking through the grass forest, he stopped and slowly looked up into the Queen Anne's lace canopy, and with a warm smile, invited Hopeful and Fearful down.

As the two climbed down from atop the Queen Anne's lace to join him, a peace came upon Fearful. He wasn't sure why, but he was glad that he and Hopeful were not alone! Helper made camp and asked them about their journey, giving them some mint tea and a fresh milkweed sandwich each.

Chapter 6

The Bonfire and the Feast

That night, Helper and the two travelers sat around a big bonfire. He taught them the reason they had felt compelled to take their journey.

"It is written upon the heart of every caterpillar the desire to seek their high purpose," Helper said.

Fearful sat by the fire and listened intently while nibbling his milkweed sandwich.

"You," Helper said, pointing to Fearful. "You knew that morning when you woke up that you must take a journey. The feeling didn't begin with you. It has been in every caterpillar since the beginning of time."

"But where does the journey lead us? Why is there so much danger along the way?" Fearful asked.

Helper sat quietly, placing another log on the fire, and answered Fearful's question. "The journey is not for the strong, Fearful, for many times, the strong think they have no need to embrace change. The journey is for those who know there is more to life than safety and peace. It belongs to those who will risk everything to discover who *Wonderful* is and what His purpose is for them in their lives."

Hopeful listened, stirring his tea and occasionally looking over at Fearful, who hung on every word Helper spoke. Helpful noticed that in the tops of the grass forest sat Mantis. They sat in preying position, keeping watch over the little party of three sitting around the bonfire in the grass forest.

Helper told them about Milkweed Way, why things must be hard, and who *Wonderful* was. "The purpose of hardship on your journey, my young friend, is to show you what is in your own heart. Only those who trust in the call within their own hearts will be brave enough to find the Beautiful Valley."

Fearful looked into the clear blue eyes of Helper, whose gaze was like the morning and soft as a spring rain.

He said to Helper, "The more words you say. the more I listen and the less afraid I feel…It fills me with comfort and joy."[12]

"Any caterpillar who sits by the flame of the bonfire and listens to my words becomes Fearless…full of Boldness and Courage," said Helper.[13]

Fireflies appeared, and old lady June bug re-appeared, sitting quietly, and writing in her scroll. She handed Fearful a lantern and Helper filled it with oil, then lit the wick with the flame from the bonfire.

"This lantern and oil will last for a large part of your journey, but there will come a time when you will need more oil," Helper said. "When your flame begins to waver, more oil will be made available to you, my little one." He handed the lantern to Fearful, looked into his eyes and said, "Be bold, and do not be afraid!"

Helper took Hopeful aside and had a quiet talk with him. "Great times of trials and danger lie ahead for you, my friend Hopeful," he said. "Remember in your time of testing what I have said. Be strong and courageous and do not let your faith waver."

Hopeful was not sure what the trails would be, but by the time they were finished talking, a new peace had come upon him. He remembered why he felt the urge to take the journey, and the words that others spoken to him.

"A Helper will come…who will teach you the things you need in order to finish the journey and remind you of the important things you have heard."

Mantis, sitting on a branch high above the group, looked at Fearful and said, "I will be praying for you, Fearful,[14] I will pray that *Wonderful* will watch over you on the dangerous journey ahead."

Fearful thanked Mantis and said he was grateful.

That night, Hopeful and Fearful felt a strange feeling come upon them. They felt renewed as they shed their skins.

"I'm all new now!" said Fearful, remembering how he had complained about shedding his skin just a few days before.

"*Wonderful* makes all things new once more,"[15] Helper said.

Fearful fell asleep and dreamed of waking up to a field of milkweed, where there were millions of other caterpillars.

Chapter 7
The Wasps

The next morning, Hopeful and Fearful discovered that Helper had gone. As they gathered their silk backpacks, Fearful noticed he had milkweed sandwiches and a new jug of mint tea in his silk backpack. Hopeful discovered the same thing and they were thrilled. They realized Helper had supplied them for the next part of their journey.

Fearful remembered Hopeful's words at the shallow pool: *"If you continue with me, not only will you regain what you've lost in the shallow pool, but you will have the opportunity to see how all your needs will be provided for!"* He decided he would no longer be afraid.

After his talk with Helper, he had found a new courage and a new strength to continue their journey. He relayed his dream to Hopeful, who gained encouragement from Fearful's words. Hopeful had also changed. He said he was beyond being Hopeful now he was "Determined."

"I didn't know words could change me so much," Fearful said. "But with Helper's advice last night, somehow I feel stronger."

Hopeful asked Fearful if he would lead the way for the rest of the trip. "Your eyes look clearer than yesterday, you have the lantern, and I feel you will know what to do and where to go."[16]

Fearful agreed.

Fearful felt an inner peace and was sure he was leading them in the right direction. As the afternoon cast longer shadows, the travelers were becoming tired. Fearful stopped in the middle of the path when he heard a humming sound.

"I hear a sound, Hopeful…can you hear it?"

Hopeful knew this sound, and it wasn't a friendly one. The sound became louder and louder. He said to Fearful, "It is getting dark. You should light the lantern, Fearful."

Before he could react, Hopeful saw a wasp swoop down and pick up Fearful. Using his backpack, Hopeful swatted at the wasp. The wasp dropped Fearful from his clutches, and this gave Fearful a chance to run into the grass forest and light the lantern.

Fearful ran back to the clearing and saw Hopeful had been caught by some of the wasps. The humming had stopped, and Fearful watched the wasp take Hopeful down the path to their camp, where they tied him up.

Not knowing what to do, Fearful wandered through the grass forest with the lantern, looking for help from other insects, and eventually, he stumbled upon the garden grubs and the slug.

"Help me, my friends! My companion, Hopeful, has been taken captive by the wasps! They have taken him to their camp! Please come and help me!"

The grubs gave him a disinterested look and continued munching the grass roots. One of them said, "Oh, we're so sorry about your friend." He munched away at a juicy root. "We will be thinking of him!"

"What good will *that* do, you lazy grubs?" Fearful asked, boldly.

Another grub looked up at him and said, "We will be sending positive thoughts your way."

Fearful left them in disgust and turned to asked the big, fat, garden slug, to come to Hopeful's aid.

"Well," sighed the garden slug, "let us consider this friend of yours and his plight."

"Consider what?" asked an angry Fearful. "He has been attacked by the wasps. We have no time to stand and talk, we must go now to rescue him!"

The garden slug licked his fingers (he had just finished eating a fat, moldy mushroom) and said, "Oh my! Those wasps are nasty fellows! Perhaps, this terrible plight has come upon him because of something bad your friend has done wrong.[17] We don't want to rob your friend of an opportunity to learn his lessons!"

Fearful screamed, "What foolish gibberish is this? My friend may die… you and I can free him if we hurry. Please help me!"

The garden slug chuckled and said, "All things happen for a reason," and then, "This too shall pass," and again, "What goes around comes around."

Fearful scowled and said to the slug, "Your empty, useless sayings won't help my friend. I'm going to rescue him myself!"

Chapter 8
The Rescue

Fearful left the grubs and the slug in the dark. He ran with the lantern back to Hopeful, as fast as a caterpillar can run. He heard the garden slug behind him continuing to quote his ridiculous sayings.

"All good things come to he who waits... Haste makes waste! A mushroom in the hand is worth two in the garden."

Fearful remembered the night before around the bonfire and the words of Helper and muttered to himself, "This certainly would be a good time for something wonderful to happen!"

As Fearful approached their camp, he was encouraged to see the wasps had only tied Hopeful's eight pair of legs together, he was gagged, and they had placed him on a suspended pole. They were sitting around in a circle, throwing dice to see who would get to attack him first.

"I threw a four and you only threw a three," buzzed one of the wasps.

"I haven't had a turn yet!" stated another.

"Whose dice are these, anyway?" asked a fourth.

Fearful counted eight wasps. They had their backs to Hopeful. Fearful circled around behind Hopeful and when Hopeful saw him, his eyes brightened.

Then, hiding the lantern so he would not be seen, secretly, bravely, and very quietly, Fearful sneaked behind the poison ivy and right up next to Hopeful. He gnawed the small spittle ropes from Hopeful's legs. Soon, Hopeful hung by only four ropes. Voices from the circle become louder.

"Ha! I got snake eyes!" shouted one of the wasps.

"You get the last roll, Spikey," said one of the wasps to the one who had not yet rolled.

Fearful knew they only had a moment to escape. Chewing quickly, he freed Hopeful's front legs. Hopeful strained against the last two ropes on his bottom feet. He finally broke the last ropes and fell free, under the ivy, where Fearful had hidden the lantern.

The wasps heard the ruckus and flew to the pole where their prey hung, but *he was gone*! They flew around in every direction, confused and angry. They flew low, looking for where their caterpillar had gone.

One screamed, "Call the others!" and suddenly, the air was thick with wasps. In the dark of the evening, there were suddenly wasps flying everywhere, looking for the caterpillar. Fearful and Hopeful crawled under the ground ivy and remained hidden there.[18] The sky immediately over the field grew even darker. It was as if a fast-moving cloud had appeared over the area and blocked out the light from the stars overhead, it helped keep the caterpillars hidden.

Suddenly, Hopeful heard a 'swoosh' and then another 'swoosh'. Fearful peeked out from under the ivy and saw what was making all the 'swooshing' sounds.

"Bats!" he cried.

Bats! Thousands and thousands of bats came swooshing down out of the twilight air, picking off first one, then a dozen, and then hundreds and hundreds of wasps out of the air. The caterpillars were shouting and hugging each other. They were saved!

Fearful said with great joy, "Isn't this wonderful, Hopeful? Isn't this wonder--" He stopped in mid-sentence. Hopeful looked at Fearful, as he finished the sentence. "*Wonderful*"? He remembered what he had said earlier: *This would be a good time for something wonderful to happen!*

Fearful now saw for himself that *Wonderful* had come, and He had come in the middle of turmoil and trouble. He had come in the time of despair and great weakness. He had come when everything seemed lost, but *Wonderful had* come, and this time Fearful had seen it!

Leaving the safety of the ground ivy, the caterpillars emerged under the night sky to discover all the wasps had been destroyed.[19] The cloud of bats had moved on and the stars twinkled overhead. While looking for his lost silk backpack, and then re-packing it, Hopeful stopped, walked over to his friend, and thanked him.

"You are not the same caterpillar I began this trip with," he said. "You came back for me, you *saved* me, Fearful! You could have lost your own life, but…" Hopeful began to weep.[20]

Fearful, felt embarrassed and tried to diminish the act. "Aww, Hopeful, I just did what you would have done!"

Hopeful raised his eyes to meet Fearful's and said, "The Silk Road has changed you, Fearful. You have traded your fear for courage, and I am in your debt, my dear friend!"

Chapter 9
The Rock Garden

Approaching the end of The Field, Fearful and Hopeful entered the Rock Garden, a very treacherous area. The Rock Garden was avoided by all the other insects because its crevices were dangerous and there were threats from their enemies. Fearful led them up, up, up into the Rock Garden, knowing it was the route they should take. The early morning sun was bright and warm.

They finally reached a plateau, and were resting in the shadows. Suddenly, several crows began circling. A brave Fearful led them further into the shadows, where they could hide. Next, they heard something behind a large rock and a deep, yet feminine voice addressed them, "Hello!" They turned quickly and found themselves face-to-face with a huge, gray wolf spider.

"What do we have here, hmmm?" asked the spider. "Two little travelers with pretty silk backpacks. Where are we going, boys?"

Six squeaky voices giggled behind the larger spider. The two travelers later learned these were her children. Their names were, Terror, Error, and Tale Bearer (they were triplets). The others were named Prideful, Spiteful, and the youngest, Hateful.

"I am Black Hole," she said. I am offering you my love and my help should you choose to accept it. I have helped so many of your brothers who have passed this way before."

Fearful's antenna spiked in the air and that told him to be cautious.

Hopeful said to her, "We really can't stay, we are going--"

Black Hole interrupted him, "To Milkweed Way. I know, my darling! I am here to help you. I know a shortcut through the rocks that will land you perfectly at the edge of the Beautiful Valley!"[21]

Hopeful felt the air spike his antenna also, and sensed great danger in her speech. He said, "We must be going!"

"Of course," said Black Hole, "but first, I welcome you to come into my den for some wonderful mint tea and milkweed sandwiches."

"They're afraid!" squeaked Prideful.

"They are ungrateful for your generosity!" said Tale Bearer.

Black Hole laughed and said, "There, there, my darlings, our friends are just very wise and careful of strangers. Aren't you my pets?"

"Y-yes!" uttered Fearful, feeling the grip of fear take hold of him again.

"We were just hiding from the crows," Hopeful explained, apologetically.

"Very wise indeed, my young friends!" replied Black Hole. "You see my darlings," she said to her children, "we can learn much from our brave friends." And with a sweeping motion with one of her eight arms, she asked, "Shall we go in for some refreshments?"

Disregarding his earlier concerns and secretly loving the idea of a shortcut to their destination, Fearful was deceived by the spider's smooth words.[22] He took a few steps into the door when a shocking sight greeted him. Just inside her door, Fearful saw *hundreds* of tiny tennis shoes thrown in heaps to the side of the room…the relics of Black Hole's previous victims. Others she had deceived.

As Black Hole began to slam the door behind Fearful, Hopeful grabbed his tiny scarf from behind and pulled him out of the den! They began running (caterpillars really can't run very fast with all those feet and little legs beneath them) toward the sunny rocks. Black Hole struggled and struggled to open the slammed door, but it had become jammed. As he struggled to free the door, Hopeful and Fearful ran for their lives.

Black Hole finally got it open and sent Terror and Error after them. The two travelers heard the steps of the two spiders behind them. As they approached the bright sunlight, Hopeful fell into a crevice and Fearful tumbled into another crevice. The spiders caught up to them and peered into the crevice, laughing at the two helpless caterpillars. As Terror approached Hopeful, the sunlight every brighter onto the rocks where the caterpillars had fallen.

The spiders shrieked loudly. Hopeful finally freed himself from the crevice and hurried over to help Fearful, who was on his back and utterly helpless.[23] Hopeful reached in and pulled Fearful out of the crevice on the far side, away from Terror and Error.

Exhausted and out of breath, they sat in the bright sunlight while Black Hole screamed, "I'll be patient my dears…I'll be patient. We spiders *hate* the light! I do my best work at night and in the shadows. Beware, young caterpillars, you *will* be my guests sooner or later."[24]

Then she slammed the door.

Fearful was the first to speak, "I am so sorry, my friend. I *knew* better, but did not listen to that new voice inside. Hopeful understood, but his face showed that he was disappointed in his friend.

Hopeful said, "There *is* no shortcut to where we are going to, Fearful. There is *never* a shortcut on the road to your purpose! We must make the trip day by day, or else our journey will end badly. *Wonderful* will not shout the hidden wisdom in times of trouble, Fearful. He speaks softly, in a whisper. You must learn to trust the whisper over the noise!"[25]

Fearful thanked Hopeful for saving his life. Fearful was about to ask Hopeful to take the lead, when Hopeful said, , "Okay Fearful, lead on!"

"You still trust me after such a mistake?" Fearful asked.

"We learn wisdom from our mistakes,"[26] Hopeful said. "You'll learn from the mistake, I trust you."

Fearful smiled and nodded. New confidence filled him and onward he went, leading Hopeful through the snags and crevices of the Rock Garden. They would sleep in the sun during the day, At night they would travel, lighting the oil lantern. The rough journey was taking its toll on the two travelers and they became weaker and wearier.

Chapter 10
The Granite Clearing

Hopeful and Fearful continued to find their way through the Rock Garden. The milkweed sandwiches Helper had provided were almost gone and the mint tea in their jugs got lower and lower. Hopeful and Fearful saw many other creatures along their way; lizards, three giant centipedes with pincher jaws, and a garden snake. They were all hungry, parched from lack of water, and looking for a meal to devour. They were not aware that the children of Black Hole were following them, hiding in the shadows.

They saw a huge scorpion whose name was Daedalus. Hopeful and Fearful had heard of Daedalus. He was the dark ruler of the Rock Garden, and all the insects were obedient to his every command.

Nighttime in the Rock Garden was the most dangerous time for Hopeful and Fearful because all the creatures they saw were night feeders. Usually, climbing into a tall plant was a safe haven for the two caterpillars, but no tall plants could be found here in this rocky place. The bright sun during the day actually worked in their favor to keep their predators at bay. They remained free from harm. and the powerful beam of the lantern given to them by the June bug, lit their way.

At night, they heard little claws scraping all around them, trying to encircle them. They knew that as long as the light from the lantern surrounded them, their enemies could not hurt them. They only needed to last one more day in the Rock Garden, and then they would come to the edge of Milkweed Way. On the last night of their journey in the Rock

Garden, the light in their lantern ran out of oil. The flame grew dim, and finally it was extinguished. Darkness encircled the two travelers.

In the darkness, the caterpillars had to pass through the Dark Valley. They came to a Granite Clearing where the steep walls encircling them was made of hard, solid granite. Hopeful saw up ahead, in the clearing, that Daedalus stood waiting..

One sting from his mighty tail killed any who tried to defy him. With his stinger coiled behind him, he was flanked by poisonous centipedes, a garden snake, and a squadron of wasps that had escaped the bats. Then they saw Black Hole and her six mischievous children.

Daedalus made a motion with one of his pinchers and a hundred fireflies, who had been tied to poles by Black Hole, were ordered to light the area. The valley was lit with an eerie green light as Daedalus stared fiercely into the faces of Hopeful and Fearful.

"Well, well…here are our two travelers, my friends!" announced Daedalus. He addressing the crowd, "These two have passed through our territory and have not paid for the privilege."

Immediately, the air was filled with shrieks, buzzing, hissing, and clicking, giving the feeling of evil.

"We, who are the true owners of this territory," continued Daedalus, "have gone hungry and thirsty, while these two have eaten milkweed sandwiches and drank mint tea."

Fearful eyed his backpack, which was now empty of any provisions. It reminded him of how hungry he was, and his stomach growled. All that was left in his silken backpack were the strange backward letters on the lining, and some empty jugs. They had not eaten for an entire day, and that, for a caterpillar, was an eternity. They were dirty, since they had not shed their skins for quite a while, their antennae were bent, and their mouths were parched. Fearful and Hopeful stood small before the assembly, as there was no exit route.

Standing between the evil assembly and themselves was a long table that appeared to have place settings on it. It seemed out of place. Daedalus saw the caterpillars' confusion and explained.

"We have watched as you both have feasted on your fine foods over these days…but you offered none to us!"

Fearful spoke, "We offered none, sir, because we did not know what you like to eat."

Laughter, shrieks, hissing, clicking, the sound of silvery wings flapping, came from the crowd that surrounded them.

"Well," said Daedalus, laughing arrogantly, "you didn't ask us!" More howls, slithering, hissing, and clicking ensued. "Since you were too...selfish to share your food with us, allow me to inform you that *you* are our food of choice!" Again, shrieks, hissing and loud clicking noises followed.

Hopeful spoke, "When we entered your territory, Lord Daedalus, we had just been provided with our provisions by a friend. We had run out of food and were hungry and tired from escaping the ants. A friend appeared...a Helper, and he gave us all the food that has sustained us while we traveled here. It was not for rudeness, sir. The food just appeared in our backpacks."

Daedalus blazed angrily, "Do you take us for fools!? Food just does not appear in silken backpacks!"

The circle of insects began to close in on the two small caterpillars, as Fearful stepped forward to the center of the circle.

Chapter 11
Fearful's Speech

Fearful heard the taunts of the insects and something within him came alive, filling him with boldness. He recognized that he had traded his fear for courage, and the feeling was very powerful. At first, Fearful tried to suppress the feeling, but he remembered what Hopeful had said:

"Wonderful will not shout the hidden wisdom in times of trouble... He speaks softly as in a whisper. You must learn to trust His whisper over the noise!"

His boldness moved him to action. He walked forward, approached Daedalus, and motioned for the assembly to quiet.

"I too, did not believe such things were possible when I began this journey. "I sought to make my own way and be in control of my world because I, just like all of you, believed that providing for my life was ONLY up to me!" Silence fell upon the assembly as he continued. "But hear me! There is one who is like the sun and like the air that surrounds us. He gives us life. His presence is enough to protect us, it is enough to provide for us…and it is enough to provide also for *you*! He does not have to obey the laws that dictate our survival, and the elements of the earth bow to His words. He is not a figment of our imagination, even if we *could* imagine such a marvelous thing."

The entire assembly was quiet, and their attention was fixed upon Fearful. There was no sound. It was as if the entire world had hushed to listen to Fearful's words. Hopeful could not believe his ears, for here, in the presence of all their enemies, the meekest and the most fearful of all the caterpillars was speaking with boldness and authority.[27]

Fearful continued, "You may wish to make us tremble with fear before you tonight, but I say boldly that even though we are small, and you are mighty, we will not bend our knees to fear. Fear no longer has power over us! We declare that *Wonderful* is our protector. *Wonderful* is our evening light and our morning star. It is He who has provided for us along our journey, and it is He who will provide for us, even now!"

With Hopeful by his side, Fearful issued a challenge, "If *Wonderful* cannot provide a bountiful table full of food for you, even now as you stand watching, then you may do to us as you please."

Hopeful's eyes grew large, realizing that Fearful was right and then, as if on cue, he continued where Fearful had left off. "However, if *Wonderful does* provide a feast, here on this table in the Granite Clearing, then you must acknowledge Him as your provider and allow us to pass unharmed."

The hissing, clicking, and flapping of silvery wings responded again to the two caterpillars. Like lightning, Daedalus' poisonous tail struck the ground directly in front of Hopeful and Fearful. "I could crush you even now!" he hissed. "I need no permission from your fairytale protector. I only need to flick my tail and you *are dead*!" He lifted his stinger and hovered it over Fearful and then Hopeful, "Shall it be him first, or you, little caterpillar?"

Neither spoke and both kept their gaze focused directly into the eyes of Daedalus. The six small spiders hid behind Black Hole in anticipation of what would happen next, and silence followed.

Black clouds gathered, and combined with the darkness. The Granite Clearing became pitch black, except for the light of the fireflies casting their eerie glow on the assembly. After a few seconds, which seemed like an eternity, Daedalus backed away from the courageous caterpillars, tilted his head back, and laughed, mocking the two caterpillars. The other insects joined in.

Black Hole mocked Fearful and Hopeful. "An imaginary feast! What fools!"

"Let's crush them now!" added Hateful, the youngest of Black Hole's children.

The laughter subsided and Daedalus stared into the eyes of the two small caterpillars. "Very well then…you have had your say. Now hear mine!" Lightning and thunder sounded in the distance as Daedalus continued, "We shall do as you have said. Let your fairytale '*Wonderful*' provide food for this table. If He does, we shall acknowledge Him and allow you to pass safely out of our land. If not, we shall eat you. … You have just five minutes."

Chapter 12

The Rain and the Banquet

As the assembly stood watching, a light, cold rain began to fall. Then larger drops came splashing down, causing a heavy downpour that threatened to drown the assembly. Small rivers of water came cascading down the granite rocks and lightning lit the sky. They were followed by loud thunder.

Hopeful and Fearful stood their ground, exposed to the downpour. The water washed over them and the dust and dirt that had covered them now washed them clean. Their bright colors were restored. Fearful stood with his head held high, but Hopeful lowered his head. Then just as suddenly as it had started, the rain ceased, and a gentle breeze followed.

Many of the insects had marveled at the rain coming so suddenly. They looked up at the sky and cowered when the lightning crashed across the sky. Even Daedalus had taken a few steps back when it began. When the gentle breeze began, their eyes once again looked at the two caterpillars who had stood their ground, and they marveled at what they saw.

Hopeful looked at the table and, saw tiny bundles appear on the plates that were on the table. Then other plates appeared, with delicacies of gnats, house flies and garden grubs overflowing on the platters that had been empty before.

Then Fearful saw it too. Fat grubs, with plates of field corn and other vegetables. The assembly slowly murmured to one another at the sight of the food. They did not believe what their eyes had seen. Clicking, hissing, and shrieking, the crowd of insects began to swell in number and crowd closely around the table.

Daedalus, who was also amazed, stood speechless at what was before him. He picked up some of the food from the table, sniffed it, and placed it back on the platter. He looked at the two caterpillars in disbelief, and was impressed that they had made neither a move nor a sound.

Daedalus broke the silence. "So be it. Let us honor our word. This…this 'Wonderful' *is* the provider!"

The entire assembly of insects repeated what Daedalus had said. "Wonderful *is* the provider! Wonderful *is* the provider!"

The insects swarmed to the table and began to feast. With a wave of his pincer, Daedalus allowed Hopeful and Fearful to fill their backpacks with Milkweed, because caterpillars don't eat insects, and motioned them toward the narrow opening behind them. They nodded in thanks and quickly walked toward the opening, but kept their eyes fixed on Daedalus. With a respectful nod from both caterpillars, Daedalus nodded back and allowed them to pass.

As they exited, Black Hole made a violent move toward the two caterpillars to destroy them. Daedalus' sharp stinger came down hard between them and her. "We will have none of this, spider!" he commanded. She retreated and the two passed through the narrow opening and left the Rock Garden behind them.

Hopeful felt something was still left to be done. He asked Fearful to wait by the olive trees and he went back toward Daedalus. "Sir?" he asked.

"Yes, caterpillar." said the giant scorpion.

"May I ask yet one more thing?"

Daedalus looked suspiciously at Hopeful. "You have escaped with your life, little one. Why do you test my patience?"

Hopeful looked intently at the giant. "The lives of the fireflies, Lord Daedalus. May they be released?"

Daedalus sniffed the air and looked at the dozens of insects, now distracted by the sumptuous feast. He motioned with his pincer, and the fireflies were released from the wooden poles. They flew away freely, leaving the feasting insects in darkness.

When Daedalus looked back at Hopeful, he bowed in respect and left.

After walking quickly for some time and realizing they had been saved once again by Wonderful, the two caterpillars lay down, exhausted, beneath a grove of olive trees.

Hopeful said, "I cannot believe your fearlessness back there, Fearful!"

Fearful began to weep, "Nor can I. It felt as if a waterfall of words were pouring out of my mouth."[28] He remembered Helper's words feeding him a few days before.

Thankfulness filled both of their hearts. Exhausted, they fell asleep, and above them, the fireflies illuminated their place of rest.

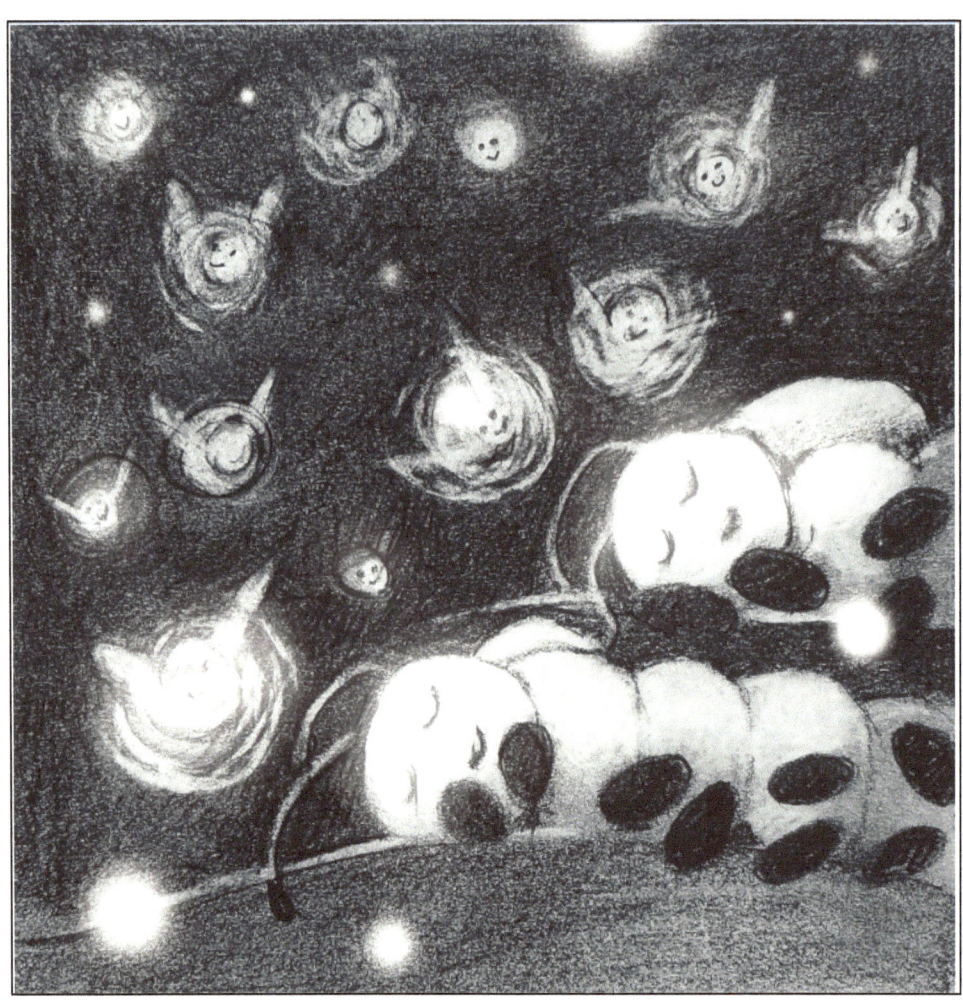

In the morning, they awakened and realized they were covered with oil from the olive trees close by.[29] Hopeful squinted, as he wiped the oil out of his eyes. He wanted to go and wash in the little river that had been created from the rain the night before. Fearful looked around and felt the air with his antenna curiously, as if it signaled trouble. His antenna swept the area and he relaxed again, as he realized the oil was not from an enemy.

It occurred to Fearful that this was the oil Helper had spoken about. Hopeful agreed, and they squeezed the oil out of their vests and backpacks, into the small container attached to the lamp. By the time they were finished, the oil lamp was full again. The light had been restored.

Chapter 13
The Fork in the Road

As Hopeful and Fearful continued walking that day, they entertained each other with memories of their adventure from the previous few days. No longer in danger, they were amused at each other as they acted out one of the scary scenes from the previous night. Fearful tried talking with a deep voice like Daedalus, at which they both laughed, uncontrollably.

A ground cricket came hopping onto their path and said, "You are the two caterpillars the whole field is talking about! You have become heroes to the rest of us, and there are stories everywhere of how Wonderful came to your rescue!"

Fearful and Hopeful thanked the cricket and continued their journey. They felt a renewed urge to get to the Beautiful Valley. Both caterpillars again felt the need to shed their skins. Each time they shed, their eyes were clearer and their desire to reach Milkweed Way grew stronger and stronger. Hopeful and Fearful talked about a common feeling they had about the changes they felt were forthcoming.

"I do not like changes," Fearful stated, matter-of-factly.

Hopeful replied, "It seems that change is the only way to prepare us for the next great challenge ahead." Still smiling sheepishly, he agreed with Fearful and said, "Although, it *would* be better to just have all the changes happen at once!"

Overhead, the tall grass forest swayed, and occasionally a cicada flew by with his soft humming of wings droning as he flew. The two continued walking and discussing the coolness of the air. It was crisper now in the morning and the wind blew gently across the field.   It made the grass forest bend over with a raspy sound, as it blew back and forth.

A calm creek flowed beside the path where Hopeful and Fearful walked. Dragonflies hovered over the banks of the small creek. The grass forest had become a tall, swaying canopy over their heads.

From time to time, the two friends climbed the tall stalks above the forest top to see what was ahead, but they could only see a short distance. The forest looked as if it stretched forever. With their silk backpacks now empty of milkweed sandwiches and mint tea, the two walked forward, ever forward, until they came to a fork in the road. One fork turned sharply to the east and the other, sharply to the west.

"Which way do we turn?" asked Fearful.

Hopeful nodded his head up and down as if to ask internally, "Which way indeed?"

The two debated the benefits of both directions and which path to follow. The path to the east looked overgrown and less easy to navigate. The path to the west looked smoother, as if it had been trampled upon by previous travelers. It was wider, but winding, with switchbacks and no straight area, making it a confusing route. The once-calm creek had become a shallow rapid, with the sound of water rushing over the rocks. After studying and discussing their options, Hopeful suggested an idea that left them both sad, but they also knew it was the only choice. He looked down at the ground, as he stumbled with his words.

"We must part from each other's company at this point, my dear friend," Hopeful stated in a sad but confident tone. "If we both choose the same path, we may both become lost. But if we separate and one of us gets to the Beautiful Valley, we can send back the dragonflies to show the other the way!"

Fearful, knowing Hopeful was right, asked him to choose the path he would take.

"Well, you are a much thinner caterpillar than I, Fearful," said Hopeful. "If I were to take the route to the west, I would be able to fit better on the path, but that would leave you with the path more overgrown, and I am concerned for your safety."

After listening to his dear friend, Fearful now spoke: "Your antenna was injured by the pill bugs, Hopeful. I feel you will have a better sense of where you are going if you take the clear path. Since I am a skinnier caterpillar, the dense grass forest will be easier for me to get through."

Logic having served them both well, they stood silently for a few moments. The weight of their decision hung heavily in the air. Sadness filled Fearful's heart. Sensing his friend's troubled heart, Hopeful considered the clear blue eyes of his friend.

"When we began this journey together, you were a different caterpillar, but as we have sojourned together, I have seen you become a brave, noble traveler whose persistence has been tested." Hopeful gulped, trying to hold back his tears. "I have learned much from you, my friend …it has been my honor to have travelled together as your companion."

Fearful could not hold back his tears. He broke down sobbing as he thought back to the beginning of their journey. "I was unwilling to take even one step more when the ants came," he stammered, "but you saw…" his voice broke, "you saw what couldn't have been seen." Fearful broke down into sobs again. "You saw the things that I could not see."

He stopped to catch his breath and to bring himself back to normal. "Your courage gave me…hope, and because of your faith, I continued on." Fearful wiped the tears out of his eyes, and regaining his composure, finally he said, "We are not meant to travel alone on most of life's journey, but I suppose there comes a time when, for at least of part of it, we must walk by ourselves, because there are decisions that we can only make on our own."

"Listen to you, my wise friend," Hopeful marveled out loud. "Just listen to you!"

The two hugged and gave each other a good-natured shove back and forth, laughing one last laugh together.

Fearful handed the lantern to Hopeful and said, "Guard the light, my friend, until we meet again."

Finally, parting ways, Hopeful said to Fearful, as he walked westward toward his chosen path,

"Resist doubt and fear, my friend. Only believe that you can make it."

Fearful shouted back, "Follow your instincts, Hopeful...they have been our good companion thus far...and they will lead you to the Beautiful Valley! May Wonderful watch over us until we meet again!"

And with that, the two caterpillars and their empty silk backpacks took their respective roads and moved forward... ever forward on their own.

Chapter 14
The Lone Journey

After parting from Hopeful, Fearful continued his walk with a heavy heart toward the Beautiful Valley and Milkweed Way. The dense grass forest made him squeeze through tight places where pigweed and gnarled vines grew. Small rocks littered the forest floor, and often he had to climb a tall stalk of grass when approaching ants stumbled along, or remained motionless when a bullfrog suspiciously eyed the landscape in search of a quick meal. In fact, his way was so difficult, he forgot for a moment about how Hopeful was faring, and instead his attention was on the potential dangers facing him.

As day passed into night, Fearful climbed a waning stalk of Queen Anne's lace to sleep, and stared out at the stars. He was tired and weak from hunger. He placed his empty silk backpack beside him as he drifted off to sleep, listening to the soft roar of the white-water creek nearby.

When morning came, Fearful was very weary and weak. He thought about the climb down the Queen Anne's lace and realized that what was once an easy feat was now quite a difficult task. He sat to contemplate his situation and knew he must climb down before full daybreak, so a wasp or bird would not grab him.

Fearful held onto the stalk with his tiny hands and feet, slowly making his way down the stalk. He had to stop many times on the way down to catch his breath. He knew that when he got to the bottom, he would have to sit and regain his strength, because he had not eaten for a very long time. He wondered how Hopeful was faring, and wished he had his friend with him right now to say positive words to him.

Reaching the bottom of the Queen Anne's lace, he sat, tired and without strength, against the stalk of a thistle. As he sat motionless, there was a sudden rustling in the grass forest. Fearful knew that he did not have the strength to move out of the way. He looked up into the canopy to see if there was any place he could escape, but he was so weak he could not move. Fearful resigned himself to perishing. The rustling became louder and louder and was coming straight toward him.

He thought again about his friend, Hopeful, and their adventures together, and said in a weak voice, "May *Wonderful*, take my friend to his destination and sustain him, for I am not able to continue."

Suddenly, breaking into the small area where Fearful sat, Helper appeared. He lifted Fearful to a rock to sit and removed two milkweed sandwiches and a jug of mint tea from his backpack. He waved them under Fearful's nose until the blue came back into his eyes. Fearful slowly came around from the smell of fresh milkweed. With a smile on his face, he said, as if he was dreaming, "Yes, Momma, I do love milkweed!"

Helper laughed and brought Fearful to his senses. He was happy to see Helper again. The two talked about the Granite Clearing, the wasps, and finally about the fork in the road.

Helper said to Fearful, "Do you remember the night we sat around the bonfire and what we spoke about?"

"Yes," he answered. "You said the journey was not for the strong, but for those who knew they only wanted to discover Wonderful."

"That's right," replied Helper. "And now it is your turn to help someone who is young, as you once were." Fearful asked him what he meant, but he only smiled and said, "I am taking care of Hopeful, my young friend." Then he reminded Fearful, "Those who wait as patiently as you have, always get their strength back! You will be running and climbing in no time, and you will not get tired as you have today. You will make long journeys and not grow faint from your adventures."[30]

Fearful overflowed with gratitude. Helper affirmed young Fearful's feelings.

"You have been brave up until now…be braver still for the journey ahead."

Fearful turned to thank Helper again, but when he looked around, he was gone. As he got up to continue his journey, once again he saw that Helper had placed lots of milkweed sandwiches and several jugs of mint tea in his backpack. Additionally, there was one other thing sitting next to his backpack. It was a lantern, filled with oil. Joy returned to Fearful and he remained there for a short time.

When he had regained his strength, he continued forward on his journey. He raised his antenna occasionally to see if he sensed danger, but not discerning any, he moved ever forward and never looked back.

Late in the afternoon, Fearful heard a faint sound, and because his journey was bringing him closer and closer to the fast-moving creek, he had to strain to be sure what he was hearing was real. Storm clouds began to gather far in the distance.

He kept making his way through the thick stalks of weed and grass, interspersed with ground ivy, stumbling occasionally as he pressed forward. He took a few more steps, pausing again when he heard a faint sound. It was the sound of someone crying. He went in the direction of the sound and discovered a small caterpillar, just like him, was sitting against a thick stalk of pigweed.

Fearful raised the lantern in the darkness of the thick grass forest, and approaching the caterpillar, he asked, "Can I help you, little one?"

The small caterpillar was frightened and began to jump up and run, but stopped when he noticed that Fearful was a caterpillar just like him.

"Who are you? Where did you come from?" asked the small caterpillar.

Fearful smiled, and asked him, "Are you hungry?" Digging into his silk backpack, he brought out a milkweed sandwich.

The antenna of the small caterpillar went up, and he began to check the air to see if there was danger lurking nearby. Seeing there was none, he accepted his offer.

Fearful spoke softly to the small caterpillar. "My name is Fearful, and

I am from a yard far, far away. I am on my way to the Beautiful Valley and Milkweed Way!"

The smaller caterpillar answered, "My name is Bentley. I am all alone… my traveling companions were all lost, some to the wasp, others to Black Hole and her children. I am the only one left and there are no others who will help me to the Beautiful Valley!" Bentley began weeping again, but this time loudly.

Fearful smiled, remembering Helper's words, that it was his turn to help someone smaller than himself. "What about me?" he asked. "I am here, and I assure you there are others, millions of others who are also going to Milkweed Way."

Bentley scratched his head with his antenna, thinking hard about Fearful's statement. "By golly, you're right!" he exclaimed, breaking into a grin. "I'm not the only one left of all the caterpillars in the world…am I? I'm going to be okay!"

Fearful told Bentley that he reminded him of someone, but he couldn't seem to remember who it was. (Bentley reminded Fearful of himself, not long ago.)

"Grab your silk backpack and come along with me then!" stated Fearful, who was now encouraged that he had a traveling companion again.

Chapter 15

The Rock Ledge

Fearful told Bentley of all his adventures, including how he and Hopeful had encountered the shallow pool, the wasps, the danger in the Rock Garden, the ants, and the fork in the road. Bentley listened with wide eyes and asked question after question. Fearful tried answering all of them, but there were so many.

Bentley finally said, with admiration, "I'm going to be like you and Hopeful!" He made a deep voice (as deep a voice as a little caterpillar could make), and acted out beating up wasps and Daedalus and trying to be a 'mighty warrior' caterpillar!

Fearful encouraged him, but warned, "Just be the caterpillar you were made to be Bentley… Hopeful and I are just ordinary caterpillars who were helped along by Wonderful and Helper."

"Even still…" continued Bentley, "I'm never going to be afraid again! You'll have to wait and see how this has inspired me!"

As they came to the edge of the grass forest, the rapids in the creek came into full view. The sound of the white water was loud, and Fearful made this his moment to announce to Bentley, "I suppose you know, my wee little friend, that caterpillars can't swim?"

Fear washed over Bentley's face, as he began to pace back and forth, wringing two of his little caterpillar feet together. He said, "Oh no, I'm too young to die! I should have stayed in the grass forest, I was happy there, I was comfortable there, I was--"

"Crying your eyes out there!" Fearful interrupted.

Bentley looked up at Fearful and said, "What will we do now?"

Fearful sat, placed the lantern close by his side, and studied their situation. "I haven't come this far to stop now, because giving up is not in my nature," he said. Looking up and down the river, he continued, "Let's make camp back in the grass forest, so as not to be seen by the bullfrogs…we will see what the morning brings."

Fearful held the lantern high because it was getting darker and darker because of the storm clouds. Crawling high into a young sapling, the pair took shelter under the large leaves of the grass forest. They heard thunder in the distance, and Fearful knew the rain was coming.

"We have to go up higher, Bentley!" he shouted over the rush of the waters and the thunder. Pointing to an outcropping of rock, he shouted, "High and dry!"

Making their way up the rock face, Bentley looked down and was frightened.

Fearful remembered the days when fear ruled him, and shouted to Bentley, "Remember, Bentley, you promised never to be afraid again!"

Upon reaching the rock table, they found a perfect hideaway from the rain that had begun to fall. Just under the ledge, they were dry and safe.[31] The storm hit so hard and lightning crashed against the ground nearby, and heard a loud "crack" accompanied by a crash.

Bentley whispered, "Everything changes so quickly… how do we know what is coming next?"

Fearful, on the verge of falling asleep, replied, "We may want to know everything that is ahead, Bentley, but something tells me we will never be completely prepared for the changes that are forthcoming."

They pushed under the rock further and fell asleep. The wind and rain pounded outside the rock ledge, but they were safe and dry.

****

The next morning, the caterpillars awakened to a blue sky and loud water flowing through the swollen rapids. Bentley looked down at the place where he and Fearful had stood the day before and saw it was completely submerged under water. He turned to tell Fearful to come and look but when he looked around, Fearful was not there!

Bentley panicked. He looked down, thinking Fearful had fallen into the water, but saw nothing. He looked to the right and the left, but again, nothing. Calling loudly, Bentley realized his voice could not be heard above the waters.[32]

When he turned around again, he saw Fearful standing at the entrance to their hideaway. Bentley felt relieved, but was upset at Fearful. "Where did you go? Could you not have told me you were leaving?"

Fearful grinned and teased Bentley. "If I didn't know any better, I would think you were afraid of something!" Fearful explained he had scouted out a crossing over the river. "That loud crack last night was from lightning that felled a tree right over the river. It's stable, but we will have to be incredibly careful or the waters will sweep us away."

"Maybe we can wait until the water goes down!" said Bentley.

Fearful said he had thought about that, but they had to press on to Milkweed Way. It was as if something told him they must go today.

"Don't be afraid, Bentley," Fearful assured him. "When you go through deep waters, Wonderful shows up! When you go through rivers of difficulty, you will not drown, and when you walk through the fire of hardship, you will not be burned up, for the flames will not consume you."[33]

"How do you know these things?" Bentley asked.

Fearful squatted down and used a stick to sketch on the ground, while he explained. "When I started this journey, I too went through the Shallow Pool. I carried everything I owned in my silk backpack, trying to save it and bring it with me, but I lost everything in the process. When you go through the water, the things that are left in the water are simply the remnants of your old life,"[34] he said, remembering the lesson he had learned from the shallow pool. "After crossing the water, you arrive on the other side, ready for your new adventures.[35]

"You cannot hold on to your life and possessions and also claim Wonderful as your provider, Bentley. It is all or nothing!"

Chapter 16
The Crossing

The two approached the edge of the swollen creek. The tree that had fallen provided a safe crossing, but they had to be careful not to slip, or they could fall and be swept away in the current.

"Remove your tennis shoes, Bentley," Fearful said. "You have better traction without them!"

Visibly shaken, Bentley removed his sixteen tennis shoes. "I can't believe I'm leaving everything I own behind me!" he said. "This isn't fair!"

Fearful looked at him sternly. "There is nothing that you leave behind that will not be made up for 100 times after we cross, but you must leave it first!" [36]

Grumbling and complaining, Bentley complied.

Fearful said he would go first to find the safe way across. He looked at Bentley, handed him the lantern, and said, "There is great power in the light of the lantern, my friend. If you become afraid while we cross, hold tightly onto the lantern."

Fearful began the crossing, making sure his little caterpillar feet were steady on the fallen log. Bentley followed closely behind him, shaking as he went. The water had made many places on the tree trunk slippery, and often, Fearful slipped and had to grab onto a branch to keep from falling in. He called behind, telling Bentley what to do. Bentley listened and obeyed the direction of his new friend.

Around three quarters of the way across the fallen tree, Fearful saw a very narrow passage between a branch and the clear final few feet to the other side of the creek. He sighed with great relief. Bentley was encouraged to see how close they were to the other side.

As Fearful approached the narrow passage, he saw movement on the other side. At first, he thought it was a leaf or a twig blowing in the wind, but then he realized it was gray and long-legged. He heard the familiar low laugh and recognized it at once as Black Hole!

Giggling, the spider jeered, "Surprise, my little travelers." She grinned widely. "I was so disappointed not to be allowed to give you and your friend a goodbye hug!" she said mockingly. She lunged at Fearful, who dodged her and crawled down, down, down, under the log, near the rushing water. Black Hole was angry and mocked Fearful. "Don't slip, my dear boy…No one likes a soggy meal!"

She pursued Fearful under the log, as the water raged around them, splashing up and threatening to wash them both into the creek below. Fearful felt the spider's legs trying to grab him. although he tried as hard as he could, he could not outrun the giant spider, who was faster than him. With one big lunch, Black Hole grabbed hold of one of Fearful's sixteen legs. He struggled to free it, but to no avail. Black Hole laughed victoriously.

"You see, my dear? Where is your imaginary protector now?" Pulling Fearful close to her stinger, she whispered, "Be still, little caterpillar…it will be quick and painless!"

Bentley could not see what was happening, since the two had climbed under the log. He sat shaking and began to cry, but he remembered the words of Fearful: "When you go through the deep waters, Wonderful shows up!"

Not knowing what moved him forward, Bentley crawled toward the log. He called out to Fearful, but heard nothing. Summoning all the courage he could, Bentley climbed down under the log where they had disappeared.

Black Hole had Fearful firmly caught, stopping him from moving forward. As she moved closer to the caterpillar, she laughed and said, "Didn't I say you would be my guest?"

Fearful looked bravely into the many eyes of the spider and quietly said, "I do not fear you!"

Black Hole smirked at him, "Enough of this foolishness! You are now *mine*!

There was movement behind Black Hole. As she turned to see what it was, Bentley held up the bright lantern and blinded her, so that she turned loose of Fearful. Still blinded by the light, Black Hole turned to attack Bentley. He turned to run back the way he had come down and under the log, as she struggled to follow close behind him. Filled with rage, Black Hole made her way back to the top of the log, where Bentley stood holding the lantern. She shielded her eyes from the bright light of the lantern and sneered at Bentley as she moved closer and closer.

Meanwhile, Fearful had climbed back up on the opposite side of the log from where he had gone down. He could only watch as Black Hole advanced toward his new little friend.

"One caterpillar is just as good as another!" she said, threatening Bentley. As Black Hole prepared to reach out and grab Bentley, two green, scissor-like arms reached out and snatched her away.

Mantis crushed the spider in his vise-like grip. In an instant, Black Hole was no more.

Fearful stared wide-eyed at Mantis, who winked at Fearful and said, "Did I not tell you that I would be praying for you, my friend? And is it not amazing that Wonderful has once again protected you?"

Fearful's eyes narrowed, as he looked intently at Mantis and nodded in grateful thanks to him.

Bentley turned and saw Fearful his friend was safe and gave a sigh of relief. The friends moved across the log to the same side, because the roar of the water was too loud for them to say anything to be heard.

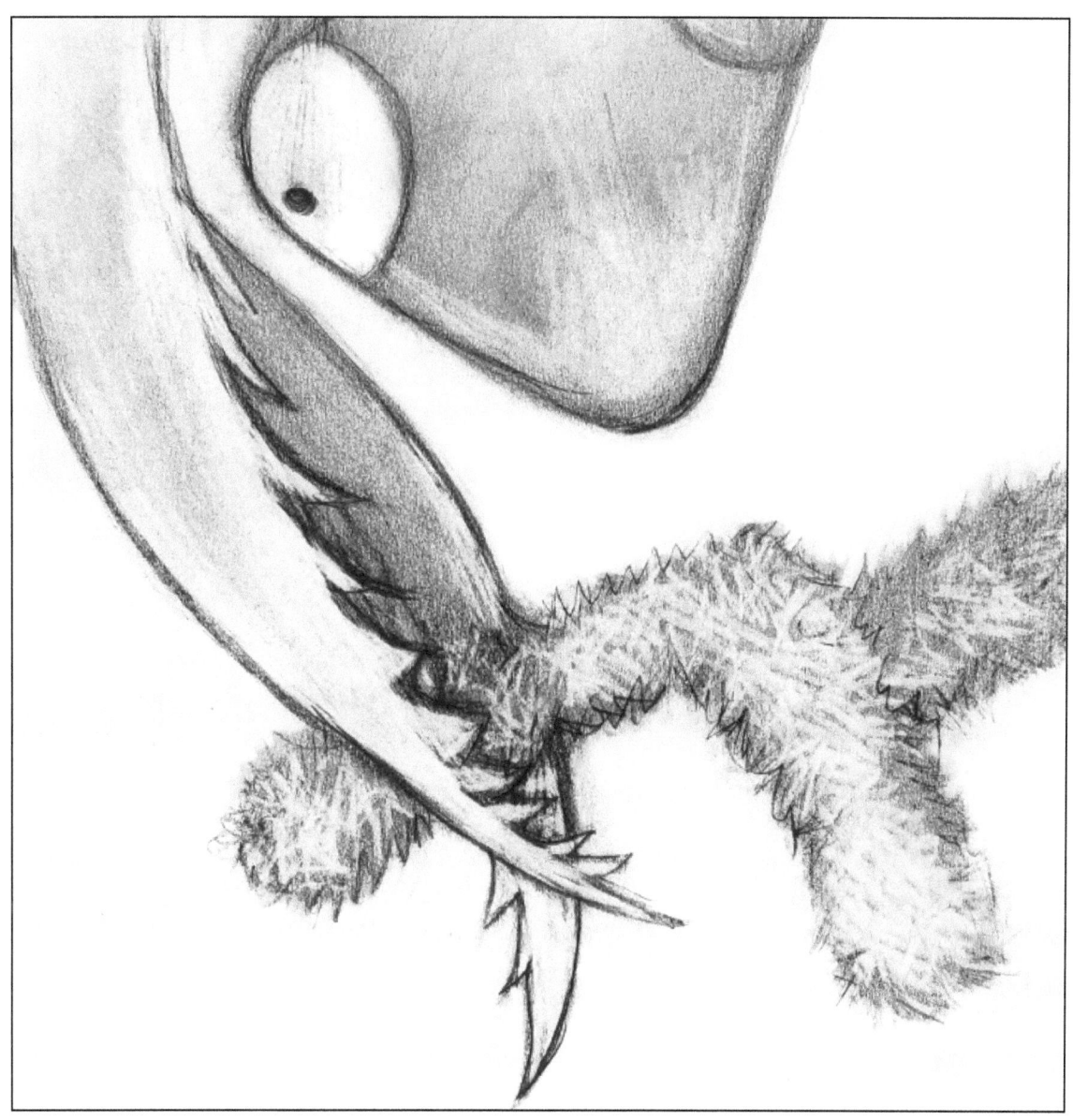

Once he reached the other side, Fearful said to Bentley, "I am so proud of you, my friend! You overcame fear and saved my life!"

Bentley smiled and said with a smile, "I told you I would be a warrior caterpillar!"

Fearful laughed, and soon he and Bentley shed their skins and their eyes became clearer. Fearful kept on the lookout and his antenna checked the air for trouble. Not feeling any danger, he opened his silk backpack, removed the two remaining milkweed sandwiches, and shared them with Bentley.

As they ate, Bentley asked curiously, "What is this gibberish written inside my backpack, Fearful?"

Fearful grinned and said, "I have no idea, little friend. But I wager there is a reason for it."

Bentley said, "The writing gets in the way of placing my other things in the backpack, since it is so thick and pushes outward. It would be too difficult for me to sleep right now. After all the turmoil we have just been through."

They moved up the bank and into the thick grass forest again.

As they approached the edge of the grass forest, the trail became wide, just as it had been at the beginning of Fearful's journey. Evening was coming soon, and they were looking for a place to camp for the night. The Queen Anne's lace was now gone, and as they walked, they heard the faint sound of music and laughter. Fearful, immediately thought of the wasps, wanting to be wary.

Bentley said with a smile on his face, "I hear clan music!"

"What's clan music?" asked a confused Fearful.

"Fearful?!" Bentley asked in amazement, "do you not know the music of our kind?"

"No, I've never even heard that our kind *had* music," replied Fearful.

Bentley's eyes cleared and he said, "The music of the clan is of old. It's a joyful sound, like a celebration of a battle already won but it's only heard in the great Congregation of the Clan."

"That explains it," answered Fearful. "I've never been in the great Congregation."

Bentley winked at Fearful and said, "Well then, there's a first time for everything!"

They walked forward carefully until they could see a large clearing ahead. It was the Congregation of the Clan... Fearful and Bentley had made it to the edge of the Beautiful Valley!

Chapter 17
The Grand Reunion

Approaching in the darkness, the fireflies flew over the two caterpillars to identify who they were, and to make sure they weren't enemies. Then they flew quickly back to the clan as they announced, "It's one of the heroes of the Rock Garden and a newcomer!" A cheer went up, and dozens of fireflies made flyover passes over the two, as they walked into the camp.

Fearful saw a bonfire and said, "There must be a million caterpillars in the camp!"

There was a beautiful green glow due to the hundreds of fireflies overhead. Bentley broke into jig to the music. He was an extrovert who talked a lot and was always ready for a party, but he could fall into despair when he was alone.

There was a lot of merriment, with many caterpillars looking and whispering to each other when they saw Fearful. Others came up and shook hands with feet and patted him on the back. Fearful didn't quite know what to make of it. Again, a cheer was raised, and mint tea flowed around the camp.

He walked in the midst of the camp, continuing to speak with other caterpillars of their journey. Out of the corner of his eye, he saw the crowd to his right part right down the middle. At first, he blinked because of the soft glow of the firefly light, but slowly, as his eyes adjusted to the green light, he saw a lone caterpillar standing in the center of the two lines that had parted...and he recognized his old friend, Hopeful!

Grinning and then shouting, Fearful ran to his friend. As they embraced, they laughed out loud, and after the hug they gave each other good-natured pokes like they had done the day they parted ways at the fork in the road. Hopeful's eyes were super-clear, and his antenna were once again straight and strong. The whole congregation offered up a

"Hurrah!" as millions of silk backpacks went flying into the air.

As if on cue, the congregation sat to hear the new stories from Hopeful and Fearful. Legends had been circulated within the congregation who arrived from near and far about the Rock Garden and all the dangers they had come through at the Granite Clearing. Many did not believe *any* of the stories since they had come through the journey without difficulty or incident.

Some of them said, "Ha! What manner of tale will these two weave?"

Still others whispered to one another, "If they are such legends, why did they go through such hardships?"

"Surely, going through hardship means you are not favored by Wonderful," they said amongst themselves.

Most of the other caterpillars, however, held them with high esteem. Fearful, looking with deep respect at his friend, sat at his feet to listen to him. Bentley, who had been drinking a wee bit too much mint tea, came staggering into the congregation with a small "burp!" The whole Congregation of the Clan laughed out loud and Bentley sat down next to Fearful, who smiled at his small friend.

Chapter 18

Hopeful's Speech

Silence fell over the Congregation of the Clan as Hopeful began speaking, in a clear voice, so that every caterpillar could hear.

"My friends and brethren," he began. "we have all come through a grand journey to arrive at this exact location and this exact time and on this exact day. Not one of us knew the perils and difficulties that would confront us as we made our way to this great valley. Some of us came with doubts within us, not knowing if we would awaken to the dawn the following day, but we all came, driven from within by an invisible urge to make this journey."

All around the Congregation of the Clan, heads nodded affirming Hopeful's words.

He continued, "We have come from near and far, and not one of our journeys has been the same. Our eyes have become clearer with every shedding of skin, and for one reason and one reason only… with the hope of the wonderfulness that is yet to come."

Claps and hurrahs rang out upon the mentioning of Wonderful.

When the clapping subsided, a caterpillar said in a loud voice, "All well and good, Mr. Hopeful, but…" he looked around at the congregation of the clan, "we all have one *real* question burning within each of us…don't we?"

The attention of the clan shifted to this caterpillar, named Dubium. He was a perpetually doubtful caterpillar, who always needed proof of something before he was ready to believe in it.

Hopeful turned to him and asked, "And what question is that, Mr. Dubium?"

Standing so he could be seen by the rest of the Congregation of the Clan, Dubium uttered the words, 'The Changing'.

A low rumbling of whispers filtered throughout the clan. Dubium sat back down, as if awaiting a reply that he would not like. Fearful knew of the Changing, as did all the caterpillars of the clan, but it was a question that he had never discussed out loud.

Hopeful stood straight as he spoke. "My friend," he addressed Dubium directly, "we all know the Changing is a part of a caterpillar's existence…a part of our daily lives. It follows that we are changed for a *reason,* and not a reason that we all will understand right now…but one that is necessary, nonetheless. The Changing is not a thing that we should fear, because we have all been changed during our journeys. Each time we have shed our skins, we have seen clearer and our understanding has become greater and greater."

He paused and looked out to the Congregation of the Clan, "I do not know the nature of the Changing, but I trust that like all things will be for our good, for the better and for the best of each of us, just as Wonderful has done for us."

The Clan was silent.

"Will it hurt?" Bentley ventured to ask, recovering a bit of his composure from the mint tea.

Giggles could be heard from the clan, with members commenting to one another, "A young one…without proper etiquette!" For it was not the proper time for a young caterpillar to question the elder.

Fearful looked at Bentley with a side glance and quietly said, "Hush, my friend, there will be time for that."

Hopeful answered his question, "All change is painful, but afterward, there is the peaceful feeling of having come up to a higher and a more powerful place[37]…the ability to accept change is wisdom, my young friend, Bentley!"

All in the congregation had recovered their silk backpacks and pulled them close. Into their midst, walked an older caterpillar. It was Helper, walking to the center of the Congregation of the Clan. The entire congregation stood as he arrived at the front. Helper, whose eyes were as blue as the bluest sky and whose face was as kind as the warmest morning, shared his words with them.

"You have been created for change, my friends. You were not born to remain an egg, nor a larva…those things were once in your future, and are now in your past. Each phase of your journey has brought you closer and closer to this day. As you have left behind your skins along the way, you will soon leave behind the present for the future."

Helper stopped to place more wood on the bonfire, As he did, the fire quickly grew. He continued, "The Changing will not come upon you from the outside, like the wind that pushes the grass forest back and forth. All changes that Wonderful perform are from within."[38] He concluded, "Tomorrow, we will all enter Milkweed Way, and as has happened up to this point, you will know what to do when we get there."

Helper turned to the Congregation of the Clan, and without a word, walked back down the center aisle he had just come up, and disappeared into the grass forest.

The sound of the wind blowing the grass forest made a raspy, rusty sound, as each of the caterpillars held up their lanterns and made their way to the encampment. They crawled up the stalks silently, to sleep for the night. Fearful drank a final cup of mint tea with his friends, Hopeful and Bentley. In the morning, they would find Milkweed Way, and discover what the Changing was all about.

Chapter 19

Milkweed Way

Morning dawned, and the Congregation of the Clan descended their stalks to begin the journey once again. Bentley sought out Fearful, who was up early and talking over the day's journey with Hopeful. Clan elders stood, speaking with a group of mantises who had arrived early for the departure of the clan. On this morning, however, something different from any other morning took place. Each caterpillar emptied out their silk backpack. No one had told them to do so. It was something they 'knew' was right to do. Seeing the empty mint tea jugs on the ground and all the personal effects of the clan, like tennis shoes, vests and the like, Bentley tiptoed over the ground to where Fearful stood.

"Can we make the journey together, Mr. Fearful?" he asked.

"I wouldn't travel without you, my friend!" answered Fearful.

Hopeful took the lead, at the head of the Congregation of the Clan, and together, millions of caterpillars began the final walk to Milkweed Way.

Dubium walked slowly, even reluctantly toward his destination. Bentley, who was not the most proper when it came to questions and the like, walked next to Mr. Dubium and greeted him with a cheerful, "Good day to you, Mr. Dubium!"

"Don't get your hopes up, boy!" snapped Dubium. "We may show up to Milkweed Way and be killed by wasps!"

Bentley's antenna raised at this response. He was testing the words, which were bitter and angry, with his antenna. He sensed Dubium's bitterness and intuitively, he remembered that many of his family and friends had perished along the journey, of which he was the only survivor. He didn't know 'how' he knew…but he knew, nonetheless.

"I lost some of my own family on my journey, sir," Bentley said respectfully. "I was left behind and alone to find my way, and if I may say so, Mr. Dubium, sir, I too was angry and bitter."

Dubium looked sideways at the caterpillar, whose eyes shone brightly and as blue as Helper's.

"If we let our losses turn us to bitterness, then we will be given to doubt, and if *that* happens, sir," Bentley continued, "then complaining and unbelief will bring the crows."

Dubium hung his head, as if to acknowledge the truth in Bentley's words. "May I be your journeyman today, sir? I feel we share a similar past, and if you don't mind me sayin', sir, I'm so proud to be your countryman!"[39]

Doubt and anger dissolved into tears and Dubium placed his hand on Bentley's small shoulder. "Such wisdom from a wee caterpillar," he said. "It would be my honor!"

From a distance, Fearful watched with admiration as Bentley, the small one, walked beside Dubium. From a greater distance still, Hopeful watched Fearful, as he watched Bentley, and was filled with gratitude.

The Congregation of the Clan walked quickly and covered the distance in a brief period. The air was now crisp, and the path widened into a lovely lane, where dragonflies droned over the clan and daisies grew on both sides of the path. Tall grass swayed back and forth on either side of the path, and at once, the Congregation of the Clan turned sharply right.

There, before their eyes, stood the largest and most beautiful field of milkweed they had ever seen! It was *Milkweed Way*! The Congregation of the Clan slowly and cautiously moved forward, each clutching their silk backpacks. One by one, they peeled them off to climb the stalks of milkweed. Hopeful, Fearful, and Bentley made a pact to climb the stalk together, and making their way to the top leaves, munched milkweed until they could munch no more.

Now, for no apparent reason, a warm wind began to blow, and the congregation was suddenly taken with a deep desire to sleep. It came on gradually. All three friends looked at the others, and for the first time in their journey, they began to knit their bottom backpacks to the underside of the milkweed. Individually, they climbed into their silk backpacks and began to knit them closed.

Before finally closing his backpack, Hopeful winked at Fearful and Bentley and said, "May *Wonderful* watch over us!"

And, into their silk backpacks every caterpillar in the Congregation of the Clan went, sewing them up from the inside, and soon fell fast asleep. The mighty throng of caterpillars that had arrived in Milkweed Way, just hours before, hung quietly in tiny chrysalises while the moon watched over the field.

Chapter 20
The Changing

Fearful grew drowsy as he lay ready to sleep in his chrysalis. Dreams of his long journey swirled in his head. He thought of his early reluctance to continue after the attack of the ants. He remembered the attack of the wasps and how he and Hopeful had slipped under the ivy to hide. Thought after thought, memory after memory, until his mind and body went quietly to sleep.

The days passed, and at times Fearful felt his body pressed against the side of the silk backpack. The bulky writing on the inside of his bag pushed against the center of his back, but he was simply too sleepy to do anything about it. Again, his dreams came, only this time his memories of the journey were getting foggy. He found it harder and harder to remember…something about a scorpion…a memory about a spider. A thick fog covered his memories.

Likewise, Bentley was no longer dreaming of losing his family and being stranded in the grass forest. He no longer remembered the events leading up to Fearful finding him. The entire Congregation of the Clan lay wrapped in a dream-like state. The fall winds blew gently with all the silk chrysalises swaying back and forth under the autumn sun.

Fearful realized his back and legs felt more and more cramped within the silk backpack. As the fourth and fifth days passed, he sensed something was happening to him, and he longed for a milkweed sandwich and some mint tea. The sun warmed his chrysalis and the outer skin of his silk backpack became thinner and thinner. As time passed, he fell in and out of sleep.

On the seventh day, Fearful heard the drone of dragonflies outside of his chrysalis and he could just make out their flight as they passed by him. He stretched and found that his legs had more strength in them. In fact, his once short, chubby legs were now longer, sleeker, and very strong! Fearful wriggled in his chrysalis, trying to get more comfortable, so he could go back to sleep, but he found himself quite cramped, as if he had outgrown it. Making one more stretch, Fearful heard a loud '**rip**' and felt the outside air rush in. The sudden rush of air brought him to full consciousness.

Without a thought, Fearful pushed and chewed at what was once the silk backpack. He made a hole in the top from which he wiggled and pushed, wiggled, and pushed, wiggled, and pushed, until finally, the top half of his body stuck out of the chrysalis. Something *strange,* of which he was unaware, was pulling him backwards.

Straining his head around to look at why his back felt so heavy, Fearful saw a sight he could not believe… he had wings! Gravity pulled at them and they began to fill out and billow in the wind. He continued to wiggle and push until his legs and feet could grasp the edge of the chrysalis, where he continued to hang for a while until his back muscles began moving his wings back and forth.

Looking to his left and right, looking above and below him, Fearful saw every member of the Congregation of the Clan appearing from their chrysalis', but they were now all beautiful, winged creatures, known as butterflies.

Bentley had emerged directly beneath Fearful. He looked up at the beautiful monarch butterfly above him and did not recognize him as his friend. He asked, "Excuse me sir, but have you seen my friend, Fearful?"

Fearful did not see him, but he recognized Bentley's voice and said,

"Bentley, surely you recognize your old friend. It's me, Fearful!"

He was not fully aware of how much he and Bentley had changed.

Bentley replied, "I'm sorry sir, but you are not Fearful." He paused. "I can see your name, and it is not Fearful!"

Fearful still hung upside down, unable to see Bentley, but said with conviction, "I am…I am your friend. And Hopeful," said Fearful, turning to where Hopeful's chrysalis hung, "hangs right over…"

Fearful stopped speaking. His eyes focused on where Hopeful's chrysalis had been. There, in his place, was a majestic monarch butterfly. Fearful chanced to call to him, "Hopeful!"

The majestic monarch looked directly at Fearful and said, "My friend!"

Laughing, Fearful said, "You have become a beautiful monarch butterfly!"

To which Hopeful replied, "Do you not realize that you also are a majestic monarch, ruling the sky with your beauty and grace?" Fearful blushed. "All who trust in the work of Wonderful become monarch rulers of the sky, my friend!"

As Fearful struggled to right himself, Hopeful told him to remain still. Fearful froze, thinking that there was a wasp or a spider ready to attack.

"Oh no, my friend." Hopeful laughed. "There is something between your wings on your back. It looks like a new name!"

Indeed, it *was* a new name. And here was the answer to the question about the writing in their backpacks. Wonderful had written their new names inside their silk backpacks, so when the Changing occurred, it would be imprinted upon them forever.[40] There in the center of the old Fearful caterpillar-turned-butterfly's back was a new, *beautiful* name.

"Y-Your name," Hopeful stuttered. "Your name is…**Fearless**"

Fearless stood still, feeling the power in his wings and legs. He read the name on Hopeful's back, "And yours is **Encourager.**" Fearless laughed.

Bentley, perturbed that he was not a part of the conversation, asked, "What is my name?"

Fearless turned slowly, and then flitted across to the next milkweed beneath Bentley to see his name. Fearless laughed and said in a proud voice, "I present to you, my monarch brethren, **Grace!**"

They all gave a loud shout, one after another, as the new monarchs called out their names in Milkweed Way.

"I am **Wisdom!**" shouted one.

"I am **Joyful!**" shouted another.

Name after name echoed down the rows and rows of Milkweed Way. Instinctively, and in an instant, thousands upon thousands of monarchs filled the sky, each flitting over the grass forest.

From where he flew, Fearless surveyed the landscape below. He saw the Rock Garden, the fallen log, the Shallow Pool and the yard…oh…he could see his beloved yard. Their wings shimmering in the fall sun, they were the last generation of the summer. This meant their lifespan would last for up to nine months! They would travel, and their wings would take them south. In the spring, they would return to their own corner of the world and start their own families.

Fearless, Encourager and Grace flew side by side. Their eyes had seen the excitement of change. They had faced danger, hardship, and death. They had battled with bitterness and fear, loneliness, and despair.[41] They had also seen that all the new things Wonderful brought to them, every trial, and every test, were filled with wonderfulness. There was never a reason to fear change. Change was a gift from Wonderful that would continue throughout their lives.

The Silk Road had indeed been a trade route. It had traded their fear for courage, their doubt for faith, their sadness for joy, and had shown the old Fearful, that Wonderful was indeed his provider.

They flew silently ahead of the Congregation of the Clan. The wind was at their backs and best of all, new adventures were ahead of them. The air was crisp, their bodies and resolve were strong and today, unlike any other day that Fearless had experienced in his life, *everything* was indeed…***wonderful!***

THE END

Author Notes

[1] *"Truly I tell you, said Jesus, no one who has left home or brothers or sisters or mother or father or children or fields for My sake and for the gospel will fail to receive a hundredfold in the present age—houses and brothers and sisters and mothers and children and fields, along with persecutions—and to receive eternal life in the age to come..." Mark 10:29-30*

[2] *"Therefore, if anyone is in Christ, the new creation has come: The old has gone, the new is here!" 2 Corinthians 5:17*

[3] *"Jesus replied, 'No one who puts a hand to the plow and looks back is fit for service in the kingdom of God.'" Luke 9:62*

[4] *"The tongue has the power of life and death, and those who love it will eat its fruit." Proverbs 18:21*

[5] *"What I feared has come upon me; what I dreaded has happened to me." Job 3:25*

[6] *"Fear of man will prove to be a snare, but whoever trusts in the LORD is kept safe." Proverbs 29:25*

[7] *"But if you fail to do this, you will be sinning against the LORD; and you may be sure that your sin will find you out. Numbers 32:23*

8 *"Some trust in chariots and some in horses, but we trust in the name of the LORD our God." Psalm 20:7*

9 *"So we fix our eyes not on what is seen, but on what is unseen, since what is seen is temporary, but what is unseen is eternal." 2 Corinthians 4:18*

10 *"But the Helper, the Holy Spirit, whom the Father will send in My name, He will teach you all things, and bring to your remembrance all that I said to you". John 14:26*

11 *"But the Helper, the Holy Spirit, whom the Father will send in My name, He will teach you all things, and bring to your remembrance all that I said to you". John 14:26*

12 *"On the last and greatest day of the feast, Jesus stood up and called out in a loud voice, 'If anyone is thirsty, let him come to Me and drink. To the one who believes in Me, it is just as the Scripture has said: "Streams of living water" will flow from within him.' He was speaking about the Spirit, whom those who believed in Him were later to receive. For the Spirit had not yet been given, because Jesus had not yet been glorified." John 7:37-39*

13 *"When the day of Pentecost arrived, they were all together in one place. 2 And suddenly there came from heaven a sound like a mighty rushing wind, and it filled the entire house where they were sitting. 3 And divided tongues as of fire appeared to them and rested[a] on each one of them." Acts 2:1-3*

118

¹⁴ *"Therefore, confess your sins to one another, and pray for one another so that you may be healed. The effective prayer of a righteous man can accomplish much" James 5:16*

¹⁵ *"Therefore, if anyone is in Christ, the new creation has come: The old has gone, the new is here!" 2 Corinthians 5:17*

¹⁶ *"For those who are led by the Spirit of God are the children of God." Romans 8:14*

¹⁷ *"He has not dealt with us according to our sins, Nor rewarded us according to our iniquities. For as high as the heavens are above the earth, so great is His lovingkindness toward those who fear Him...." Psalm 103:10-11*

¹⁸ *"Whoever dwells in the shelter of the Most High will rest in the shadow of the Almighty." Psalm 91:1*

¹⁹ *"You will not have to fight this battle. Take up your positions; stand firm and see the deliverance the LORD will give you," 2 Chronicles 20:17*

²⁰ *"Greater love has no one than this: to lay down one's life for one's friends" John 15:13*

²¹ *"...for Satan himself masquerades as an angel of light" 2 Corinthians 11:13-14*

22 *"With persuasive words she led him astray; she seduced him with her smooth talk. All at once he followed her like an ox going to the slaughter, like a deer stepping into a noose, till an arrow pierces his liver, like a bird darting into a snare, little knowing it will cost him his life." Proverbs 7:21-23*

23 *"The path of the righteous is like the morning sun, shining ever brighter till the full light of day." Proverbs 4:18*

24 *"Stay alert! Watch out for your great enemy, the devil. He prowls around like a roaring lion, looking for someone to devour." 1 Peter 5:8*

25 *"So He said, 'Go forth and stand on the mountain before the LORD.' And behold, the LORD was passing by! And a great and strong wind was rending the mountains and breaking in pieces the rocks before the LORD; but the LORD was not in the wind. And after the wind an earthquake, but the LORD was not in the earthquake. After the earthquake a fire, but the LORD was not in the fire; and after the fire a sound of a gentle blowing."*
1 Kings 11-12

26 *"Even though Jesus was God's Son, he learned obedience from the things he suffered." Hebrews 5:8*

27 *"When they saw the courage of Peter and John and realized that they were unschooled, ordinary men, they were astonished and they took note that these men had been with Jesus." Acts 4:13*

²⁸ *"Whoever believes in me, as Scripture has said, rivers of living water will flow from within them." John 7:38*

²⁹ *"Behold, how good and how pleasant it is For brothers to dwell together in unity! It is like the precious oil upon the head, coming down upon the beard, Even Aaron's beard, coming down upon the edge of his robes...." Psalm 133:1-2*

³⁰ *"...but those who hope in the LORD will renew their strength. They will soar on wings like eagles; they will run and not grow weary; they will walk and not be faint." Isaiah 40:31*

³¹ *"The name of the Lord is a fortified tower; the righteous run to it and are safe." Proverbs 18:10*

³² *"Therefore, let everyone who is godly pray to You in a time when You may be found; Surely in a flood of great waters they will not reach him." Psalm 32:6*

³³ *"When you pass through the waters, I will be with you; and when you pass through the rivers, they will not sweep over you. When you walk through the fire, you will not be burned; the flames will not set you ablaze." Isaiah 43:2*

³⁴ *"We were therefore buried with him through baptism into death in order that, just as Christ was raised from the dead through the glory of the Father, we too may live a new life." Romans 6:4*

^{35} *"I have been crucified with Christ and I no longer live, but Christ lives in me. The life I now live in the body, I live by faith in the Son of God, who loved me and gave himself for me." Galatians 2:20*

^{36} *"And everyone who has left houses or brothers or sisters or father or mother or wife or children or fields for my sake will receive a hundred times as much and will inherit eternal life." Matthew 19:29*

^{37} *"No discipline seems pleasant at the time, but painful. Later on, however, it produces a harvest of righteousness and peace for those who have been trained by it." Hebrews 12:11*

^{38} *"…nor will people say, 'Here it is,' or 'There it is,' because the kingdom of God is in your midst." Luke 17:21*

^{39} *"The Spirit of the Sovereign LORD is upon me, for the LORD has anointed me to bring good news to the poor. He has sent me to comfort the brokenhearted and to proclaim that captives will be released and prisoners will be freed." Isaiah 61:1*

^{40} *"To him who overcomes I will give some of the hidden manna to eat. And I will give him a white stone, and on the stone a new name written, which no one knows except him who receives it." Revelation 2:17.*

^{41} *"Persecuted, but not forsaken; cast down, but not destroyed; Always bearing about in the body the dying of the Lord Jesus, that the life also of Jesus might be made manifest in our body. For we which live are always delivered unto death for*

Jesus' sake, that the life also of Jesus might be made manifest in our mortal flesh."   *2 Corinthians 4:9-11*

Author Bio

Douglas Pacheco is a writer, speaker and storyteller who is passionate about recognizing opportunities and taking advantage of them in order to share the love of Jesus with others.

He is a former pastor and missionary. He resides near Nashville, Tennessee with his wife Mary Ann.

Douglas writes a daily blog at www.unremarkablemiracles.com.